Yo
trending
in my dreams

Also by the same author

You're the Password to My Life

Sorry, You're Not My Type

It Started with a Friend Request

That's the Way We Met

Few Things Left Unsaid

You're trending in my dreams

Sudeep nagarkar

RANDOM HOUSE INDIA

Published by Random House India in 2015
Third impression in 2015

Random House Publishers India Pvt. Ltd
7th Floor, Infinity Tower C, DLF Cyber City
Gurgaon – 122002
Haryana

Random House Group Limited
20 Vauxhall Bridge Road
London SW1V 2SA
United Kingdom

978 81 8400 671 1

Typeset in Requiem Text by Manipal Digital Systems, Manipal

Printed at Replika Press Pvt. Ltd, India

A PENGUIN RANDOM HOUSE COMPANY

To those who tussle for the last slice of
pizza with their friends!

Bade ajeeb hai ye zindagi ke raaste,
Anjaane mod par kuchh log dost ban jate hain . . .

Contents

Prologue

Life is like a road full of twists and turns. All you have to do is learn how to drive in such a way that your close ones are protected. You might be as hard as a nail but there is always that one person in your life you are willing to give a second chance to. She was one of them.

Varun and the others had accepted the grave mistake she had committed without pulling her up.

'Did you take your medicines?' he asked in concern.

There was no response from her. She looked traumatized and fiddled with her mobile phone to distract herself from the agony of her recent experience.

'I am asking *you*. Did you take your medicines?'

'No,' she replied bluntly.

'Will you put your goddamn phone down and explain what the matter is?'

'Fine. You want to hear my side of the story? I surrendered to the situation. I know I'm partly at fault but I can't face the consequences. I feel like a trap was set for me and I've fallen headlong into it. You don't trust me, do you?'

She had tears in her eyes as she looked at him and put her mobile phone aside.

'It isn't just me, the others trust you as well. But this is just not the right way to behave. I thought you were stronger than this,' he said, trying to console her.

She was about to say something but the pain in her head had become unbearable. This was not an unfamiliar pain. Suddenly, the haunting memories of her past that she had kept hidden away came rushing back.

Varun stroked the back of her head to comfort her. Just as she was about to take a breather, her phone beeped. The screen displayed an unknown number, but the voice on the other end was not unknown. She started shivering. She couldn't manage to speak a word.

'I will expose you. If you don't believe me then you can check your WhatsApp messages.'

The phone got disconnected. With a heavy heart, she managed to look at the mobile screen.

'1 WhatsApp message received.'

It read, *'You have just 2 choices. Do as I say or face the consequences.'*

A few pictures and a video accompanied the message. What had happened a few days ago was a mere trailer compared to what she saw in this message. Varun tried asking what was happening but she was devoid of any emotion. She looked dazed. He snatched the phone from her and what he saw shattered the ground beneath his feet.

The demons she thought she had left behind had come back to haunt her. They left her feeling exposed and vulnerable. She shivered and withdrew under her sheets. What was she running away from? And how soon will it be before her demons caught up with her?

Women are considered more fragile but nothing is as easily wounded as a man's ego. It was a man's bruised ego that had created such a mess in her life!

While she tried to get some sleep, her roommates speculated on what to do next. No one wanted her to give in to the caller's demands.

What do you do when you don't even know what you want for yourself, because you have always been doing things for others?

Fourgasm—Four People, Four Lives

'Varun . . . *Varun* . . . where the hell have you been? Do you take me for a fool?' Varun's dad asked in an aggressive tone.

'I don't care. I don't give a shit about your nonsense. You are a drunkard and it's my misfortune that I have to call you Dad,' Varun responded with equal aggression from his room where he had locked himself in. The father–son relationship had been strained ever since his mother passed away when Varun was still a child.

Varun was fair-complexioned, with light brown eyes and a slight stubble. He was extremely fond of branded watches and had a huge collection of them. He was very possessive about his watches, and would never allow anyone to even touch them. Girls in his college would go gaga over him but no one mustered the courage to speak about their feelings to him as everyone knew how strict his dad was.

His father was an ex-army officer and, post his mother's death, he was brought up in a strict military-style environment where there were 'rules' for everything. His father had retired from the military a couple of years ago but still bossed people around. But Varun hated being trapped in the confines of his home. He loved to explore and take risks. There was a flip side to it though. Every time he did something reckless, he would get a beating from his dad. Things didn't end there. His father would shoot the choicest expletives at him and torture him mentally when he was drunk. All this was slowly making Varun retreat into a shell. He had changed from the jovial person he was to a person with limited interactions with the outside world.

Varun dreamed of running away from the cage his dad had built for him. He always felt from his father's attitude that he never really loved him and that realization made him miss his mother even more. He would pen down his innermost thoughts in a diary whenever he could. But he was no writer or anything. His desire was to one day become an entrepreneur and do as his heart desired rather than opting for a job and be enslaved by a handful. He believed in the adage 'It's not about the ideas, but making ideas often'.

'Come out, you son of a—' his dad shouted yet again.

But before he could finish, Varun yelled from inside, 'Mind your tongue! And lay off me!'

The reason for their heated discussion was that Varun wanted to shift to Mumbai to pursue BSc and had even applied for the course but his dad wanted him to join the army. Varun wanted to do as he pleased and was not going to let anything come in the way of his ambitions—least of all his father. He picked up the phone and called his friend Ahana in frustration.

'That's it! I just can't take it any more. I want to run away from all this nonsense,' Varun complained.

'Why don't you come over and stay in my flat in Mumbai? A couple of other girls are sharing it with me and I am sure they won't mind if you join in. Of course, that's if you feel safe with three girls around you.' She laughed.

'That's awesome! I will carry my headphones along so that I don't have to listen to all your girl talk,' Varun teased.

The conversation relieved his frustration to an extent and helped him make up his mind—to run away to Mumbai and join the BSc course he had applied for.

'I'm only worried that once your parents find out, they might inform my dad about me staying in your apartment,' Varun said.

'Don't worry. My dad won't bother. Your dad at least cares to throw you a slap or a few harsh words. My dad just throws some money into my account every month and thinks he is done,' she added.

'Let me think about it some more,' Varun replied.

'It's your choice at the end of the day. But I seriously feel you need to get out of the shithole that you call home. Please. Just do this for me, if not for yourself?'

'All right. You're such a good friend, Ahana. I'm glad to have you in my life.'

After the brief discussion over the phone, Varun ended the call. It was final now—he was going to shift to Mumbai without fearing the consequences. He was all set to checkmate his dad's violence and break free from the cage of restriction. He was going to move into the apartment rented by his friend Ahana!

One month earlier

'Dad, I've secured admission in NIFT, Mumbai, and college begins within a month. Finally I'm going to live my dream of becoming a top fashion designer,' Ahana exclaimed in excitement.

Ahana was full of life and passion. She enjoyed late night parties and lived the life of a princess even though she was still in school since her dad was a rich Delhi-based businessman. She was a real beauty—fair and flawless skin, sparkling eyes that expressed thousands of emotions and a smile that could bring the world to a standstill. She loved shopping and was extremely brand conscious—only wearing the best brands like Zara and Forever 21. The tattoo on the side of her neck added to her charm. It showed the world that she had a modern and independent outlook. She had grown strong, building a firm foundation with the bricks thrown at her.

She wanted to be one of the top fashion designers in the country and her dreams meant the world to her. Often we come across people who are constantly trying to make others around them happy. But when we look deeper at them, we find that such people are pretty lonely themselves. She was one of them. Though she was quite the social butterfly, she had only a handful of trustworthy and close friends including Varun, who happened to be the son of her father's close friend.

She always sought attention and love from her dad but all she ever got was money. She still had immense respect for him but somewhere she missed the paternal love that every child yearns for. The way a father treats his daughter shapes how she views herself and how she expects to be treated by other men around her for the rest of her life. Her father had never expressed his fondness for her and so she never took men seriously. Neither did she care about getting into a romantic relationship. She just lived in the moment.

So when she excitedly told her dad about having secured admission in Mumbai, she expected him to get excited as well. However, he continued to work on his iPad without bothering to even look up. She thought that he might get up and hug her. After all, every girl wants her dad to be with her in all the good times and shower her with love and praise.

'Congrats! I will transfer the money for your fees. You can stay in our flat in Mumbai. No need to look for a hostel,' her dad replied with his eyes glued to the iPad.

'Okay, Dad,' Ahana replied and went to her room in a dejected state.

When a father ignores his daughter, she spends her life trying to replace him in her heart. If he is warm and nurturing, she will look for a lover to equal him. If he thinks she is beautiful, worthy and feminine, she will be inclined to see herself that way.

Ahana had accepted her dad the way he was. In Ahana's case, it was not that her dad didn't appreciate her, but work pressure didn't allow him to spend enough time with her as she was growing up. However, she was strong and her strength didn't come from lifting weights—it came from lifting herself up whenever she was knocked down.

In the next couple of days, she shifted to her own flat at Sea Woods, Navi Mumbai, though there were still a couple of weeks left for college to begin. She wanted to get used to the 'Mumbai Way of Life'. Plus she wanted to look for a roommate to stay with because she didn't want to live alone and the idea of having a roommate excited her. She advertised online as there were many colleges in Navi Mumbai and students do look around for shared rooms. But she didn't find an appropriate girl for over a week. After a fortnight, her routine began and she gradually settled down to her new life. She still continued to splurge on unnecessary things as her father would transfer enough money into her account every month. The search for a roommate finally came to a close when she bumped into a girl named Malvika at the gym where she exercised. Malvika too was looking for a room nearby and Ahana took an instant liking to her.

'Ahana, will there be room for another girl to join us? I have a friend who is looking for a place to stay. Her name's Garima. Are you okay with her moving in with us?' Malvika asked one day at the gym before accepting Ahana's offer.

'Absolutely fine. You can both shift tomorrow itself. I am sure we will have a blast staying together,' Ahana winked.

The next day, Malvika and her friend Garima shifted to Ahana's apartment. Ahana had made it clear to Malvika that she was a party buff and drank on weekends. Malvika was all too pleased upon hearing this since she too loved to party and drink. Though Malvika's friend was the opposite of her, she was pretty cool when it came to things like this.

You will never find someone who is perfect. Everyone has their issues; the trick is to find someone with issues you can deal with. As time passed, they had learnt the trick to give each other the freedom to be who they really were.

It was a weekend when Ahana received Varun's call. They had hardly talked after Ahana shifted to Mumbai.

'Hey, how are you?' Ahana asked.

'Everything's terrible. Worst of all, you seem to have forgotten me,' Varun added.

'Shut up, you asshole. Tell me what's bothering you now. Must be your dad. What else!' she laughed.

'I just can't take it any more. I want to run away from all this nonsense."

'Didn't I tell you to come over and stay in my flat in Mumbai? Don't worry. It's going to be fine,' she said.

Their conversation continued for some time until Varun made up his mind to shift to her flat. She put the phone down and waited for Malvika and her friend to return from college. She wanted their opinion on Varun's situation and whether they were comfortable with having a guy move in with them.

It was while having dinner that Ahana brought up the topic. They had a detailed discussion about it and Ahana assured both of them that Varun was a trustworthy and genuine person.

'There is no reason to fear. You can trust me and I assure you guys, you will love his company too,' she said.

'What about the neighbours? What if they come to know about it?' Malvika added.

'I don't give a damn about the neighbours. It's my house, so who are they to decide who I should stay with?' Ahana said firmly.

'I am cool with it. Is he hot?' Malvika asked with a mischievous grin.

'Totally!'

Malvika laughed and they gave each other a high five. Living together with a guy was a thrilling idea. She had no objection to sharing a flat with a guy; in fact she was pretty excited about it. However, her friend Garima was a bit worried, not because she was orthodox or old-fashioned, but because of her own circumstances. Her past experiences had made her keep her distance from everyone. She took her own time to get comfortable with new people. And the idea of living with a guy didn't excite her at all.

However, Malvika convinced her that it wouldn't be such a big deal and that she was always there by her side, so she had nothing to fear! Garima finally gave in.

Two weeks earlier

'Why did you upload such a depressing status on Facebook? There is no point in sobbing over the past,' Malvika chided. Her friend Garima had just updated her Facebook status with: *Time will heal the haunting memories of the past . . . but will never completely erase them.*

Malvika was a Mumbaikar who had taken admission in DYP Dental College, Nerul, Navi Mumbai. As her home was at a considerable distance from her college, she preferred to stay in the college hostel to save on travelling time. She was mature enough for her age, compassionate and caring. She was the girl you'd rather talk to in bed than take to bed. Hot girls play with your heart, decent girls mend it. She knew how to speak her mind intelligently and captivate others with her words and opinions. Her words were what made her the woman she was, enchanting and dreamy. Her beauty radiated from the purity within her that made her look effortlessly beautiful. Her dimples made guys go gaga. She wanted a guy who could touch her heart and soul.

'It's true, Malvika. Even though time will heal the painful memories of the past to a certain extent, it will never completely erase them. And anyway, what's the point of raking up past issues when no one believes me? Not even my own mom,' Garima muttered in a sad tone and eventually changed the subject.

Malvika wanted to know more about Garima's past to ease her pain but preferred not to probe too much as it might hurt Garima more that doing her any good. It was the second week of college. Malvika and Garima had met on the first day and had become friends instantly as they shared the same hostel room. Garima was from Madhya Pradesh and had shifted to Mumbai for the same dental course as Malvika's. A chubby, sweet girl who was an introvert, she was not shy or meek but she preferred not to go out for reasons better known to her. Since she was still a virgin, she was often taunted by her classmates. Her circumstances had shaped her personality in a certain way and though she tried to be more outgoing, it was genuinely difficult for her to be so. She was not at all old-fashioned but preferred to stay away from relationships and be with a limited set of people with whom she was comfortable. Surprisingly, she gelled very well with Malvika and they soon became good friends. Bored with the tasteless hostel food they were served day in and day out, they decided to search for a PG near college. It would also mean freedom from the restrictions that came with staying on the hostel premises.

Luckily for them, an opportunity arrived soon after, when Malvika made friends with Ahana at the gym and Ahana started to discuss her flat-hunting problems. 'That's perfect,' Malvika exclaimed. 'I have been looking for a place to stay and this works out just fine.' Malvika mentioned getting another friend along to stay with her and Ahana assured her there would be enough room for all three of them. Once Malvika reached home, she shared the news excitedly with her friend. 'Garima, I told you about my gym friend Ahana, right? Today we were just talking casually and I told her that we are looking for a PG. Guess what? She was looking for flatmates for her apartment and is okay with us moving in.'

'Me too?'

'Yes. I told her that we both are looking for a PG and she was absolutely fine with it.'

'Awesome. At least now we can have proper food. This mess food sucks,' Garima said, making a face.

'Not only food, darling, we can have all the fun we want without any hostel warden dancing over our heads all the time. Plus she is the same age as us and so we will have complete freedom unlike a PG where there are so many restrictions—no booze, no late nights. Now we are free to do as we please. That's what I call life.'

'You know I don't drink. But I am happy that we can now live life as adults and eat better food than this rubbish at the mess.'

The next day they completed the hostel formalities and were all set to shift to Ahana's apartment. Sometimes girls are weary of each other and sometimes they become thick friends. Gradually, all of them had learnt to respect each other's thoughts and beliefs. Sometimes they laughed together and sometimes they cried. Sometimes they fought and sometimes they persuaded each other into doing silly things. As weeks passed, they knew almost everything about each other and even though Garima was of a reserved nature, she still loved Ahana and Malvika's company. They helped her slowly open up to them. Even though they had their faults, they loved each other and all of them believed 'Friends are forever, boys are whatever'.

When Malvika and Garima returned from their extra classes in college, Ahana brought up the topic of Varun shifting to their apartment. She told them everything that they needed to know about him and everyone agreed eventually.

'It's going to be a thrilling experience to stay together then.' Malvika smiled, looking at Garima who was still slightly sceptical about a guy coming to stay with them even though she had agreed to go along with the entire idea.

When people are meant to be together, no matter what the relationship is, no matter how far apart, the universe will always find a way to bring them together. Varun, Ahana, Malvika and Garima were meant to be together. We can never choose the way life is going to turn out but we can choose the way we spend each moment. Four people with different dreams had decided to stay under one roof. Friendship is a two-way street and requires effort from both sides. How strong was their friendship going to be—only time would tell!

Friends Are Forever, Boys Are Whatever

It was a lazy Sunday morning. Without a care in the world, the three girls were fast asleep in their respective rooms. Suddenly Ahana's phone beeped. It was Malvika. For a moment Ahana thought that Malvika was not at home and asked, *From where are you texting?*

Malvika: *From my bedroom.*

Ahana: *What do you mean??*

Malvika: *I mean I am inside my bedroom and too lazy to get up and come out.*

Ahana: *You are such a bitch! I was in the middle of a beautiful dream when you texted.*

Malvika: *I am going to order some healthy breakfast today. I seriously need to start eating healthy. Have piled on so many kilos eating outside food.*

Ahana: *Bitch please. Spare me and go to sleep. And DND.*

DND was of course short for Do Not Disturb.

Good girls are made of sugar and spice, but these girls were made of vodka on ice.

After a few hours of lazing around in her bed doing nothing other than Facebooking, Malvika sneaked into Ahana's room and picked up a packet of potato chips from Ahana's bedside table. Ahana had planned to dig in to it while watching *Gossip Girl* or *Friends*.

Ahana woke up to see Malvika eating the chips and yelled, 'Put those aside. I had bought them for munching on later. And madam, you were supposed to eat healthy, right?'

'Calories don't count when it's your roommate's food,' she winked.

'Such an ass you are.' Ahana threw a pillow at her.

Garima got up to ask why they were shouting. Ahana pointed towards the so-called 'healthy food' Malvika was binging on.

'Yes, she always eats healthy. Yesterday she ate more than half of my BBQ chicken pizza with extra cheese.' Garima laughed as she kicked Malvika from the back.

Finally, everyone gave up on the idea of eating healthy and Garima decided to make pasta for lunch.

In the meantime, Ahana was busy clicking selfies in front of the mirror to upload on her Instagram account.

'What's with the sexy pose? Are you clicking selfies to seduce someone?' Malvika teased her.

'Darling, I don't need to seduce anyone. Guys surrender with just one glance from me.'

'Oh please.'

'That's Ahana for you, sweetheart.' Ahana laughed.

Malvika went close to Ahana and started rolling her fingers down her neck as if seducing her. Both of them pouted in front of the mirror and clicked pictures like models posing on the ramp at Lakmé Fashion Week. They took off their tops and clicked a few more selfies in just a bra and shorts. Of course, these pictures were for their own personal fun and not to be uploaded on Instagram.

'Are mine a good size?' Malvika asked, pointing towards her boobs and comparing them with Ahana's in the mirror.

'They are perfect. Now stop behaving like lesbians and come out for lunch!' Garima screamed, standing by the door and gesturing at them to come out.

'You want to join us in our selfies? We will upload them and make everyone jealous,' Malvika asked.

'If I join, it will not be a selfie. It will be a groupfie.' She winked and added, 'Anyway, if you point the camera away from yourself for once, you just might find someone interesting on the other side.'

'Don't start your psychology class again.'

The pasta was amazing and everyone pounced on it. Once done, they started watching an episode of *Friends* where Monica asks Chandler, 'Do you want our guy to be your guy?' which made Ahana inquire about Malvika's previous relationships.

'I just wished we could have taken it slow for a little bit. You know, I just wish we could be like . . . on a break . . . and I could just do whatever I wanted to back then,' said Malvika, reminiscing about her relationship.

Ahana laughed and asked Garima about hers.

'I am not ready to be in a relationship just yet,' Garima stated.

Malvika realized Garima was not comfortable answering questions about relationships and butted in. 'I will date your guy only if he smells incredible. Else he can buzz off. Tell me about your first kiss. Was it as good as they show in pictures and novels?' Malvika asked Ahana.

'I don't take relationships seriously. But my boyfriend was really dumb in the beginning. We used to take the same salsa class and once while practising I whispered in his ears that I was thirsty and needed something to drink. He guided me towards the filter. He was a geek, I guess. He couldn't understand my signs. When the practice was over and we were in his car driving back home, I gave him a seductive look and held his hand. I told him to slow down at the corner of the road as it was dark. For a moment there was silence and then he started explaining about the music system in his car. His constant blabbering pissed me off. I simply moved towards him and thrust my body upon him. "You are too dumb to handle hints," I said and smooched him deeply. He was completely shocked. Maybe we should have watched porn first to get him more comfortable.'

Malvika couldn't control her laughter upon hearing this. Their gossip continued for some time. Garima was enjoying all the fun even though she didn't participate in the discussion much.

'What ridiculous things have you done in a relationship?' Ahana asked Malvika.

'I would secretly spy on my boyfriend and if I found him flirting with another girl, I would do the same with other guys just to grab his attention. I hated all his female friends for no reason. I would tell him I was jealous of his other female friends but would add "just kidding" to the sentences I actually meant because I didn't want to hurt him. I used to read his messages when alone. After our break-up there were so many songs that would remind me of him and I totally loved it when he tried to make up after a huge fight. I had even planned my wedding, kids and life with him but things don't always go as per plan. Now I feel that it was just an attraction, nothing else,' Malvika stated.

Though the three of them were away from home, they had created such a strong bond with each other that it felt like a family. Things would have gotten really lonely otherwise. They talked trash, they laughed and even cried together—it was the kind of therapy that money can't buy. Friendships are what make us strong when we feel weak, happy when we feel sad and comforted when we feel alone.

'Ahana, are you leaving?' Malvika asked.

'Yes. In some time,' she answered from the bathroom.

Ahana had to meet her boyfriend Sid and was about to leave. Malvika was removing her clothes that were drying on the clothes line in the balcony when suddenly her bra fell down at the feet of a man who lived in the same society. He instantly started screaming at the girls.

'Don't you have any shame? You girls ruin the culture in the society by coming late at night in a drunken state and now you can't even take care of your underthings!' He pointed at the bra fallen on the ground as he shouted at them.

Ahana heard him yelling and came out running from the washroom. 'That must be Verma for sure. Today I'm going to teach him a lesson and make sure he never messes with us again,' she muttered under her breath.

Meanwhile Verma continued, 'I am going to complain about you girls at the next society meeting. I will not take it—'

Before he could complete his sentence, Ahana came to the balcony. This was not the first time such an episode had occurred. Earlier too he had created a scene and Ahana had shut him up.

'Oye, Mr Chutiye, did your mother not teach you how to talk to girls? And does your wife know about your affair with the bhabi next door? Should I tell her what you are up to when she goes for a walk in the evening? Bloody rascal, now you will teach us how to behave?'

Mr Verma didn't expect Ahana to do such straight-talking. The girls rejoiced as he bowed his head in embarrassment and walked away.

'Don't listen to such perverts. If you act weak in front of these people, they will dominate you. Now he will never dare to mess with us again. Remember this always,' Ahana explained to Malvika.

'I understand. But what about my bra? It's still lying on the ground!'

All three of them looked at each other and broke out laughing. Ahana was smart and bold enough to speak her mind without fearing the consequences. She knew how to deal with tough situations on her own. She was not a woman who needed a man—she was a woman a man needed!

After the incident, she left for Belapur in her car to meet Sid. He was a gym trainer who had completed his American College of Sports Medicine certification in personal training and was working with Red Gym in Sea Woods. Ahana and Sid had met at the gym a few weeks ago when Sid had been assigned to train Ahana. His good looks and well-built physique had attracted Ahana and they became close during the training sessions. Sid knew Ahana came from an extremely rich family and didn't want to miss an opportunity to date her especially since she lived away from her parents. It was just a passing affair but as each day went by, Sid became more serious about the relationship and wanted to sustain it.

Ahana reached the lounge where Sid was waiting for her.

'You look gorgeous,' Sid exclaimed, admiring her red tube top and black skirt.

Being an aspiring fashion designer, Ahana knew how to put a good outfit together. She smiled and gave him a warm hug as they went inside to the more private section of the lounge on the upper floor. Grabbing their seats in a corner of the lounge, they ordered a mint-flavoured hookah along with some French fries.

'What is the secret to your beauty? I can just look at you for hours,' Sid said admiringly.

'Stop being so filmy.' She smirked.

He went closer to her and slowly moved his hand up her thigh. There was no one on the upper floor and they had all the liberty to do as they pleased. He held her by her waist and gave her the wildest kiss ever. Ahana moved her hands over his pants and moaned. They were so engrossed in each other that they didn't even see the waiter standing by with the hookah and a wicked smile on his face. Ahana hurriedly pulled down her skirt while Sid sat up straight. After placing the hookah on the table, the waiter remarked, 'You can continue,' before leaving.

Ahana maintained a distance this time as they enjoyed the hookah, exhaling smoke rings. Ahana wanted to inform Sid that her friend Varun was soon going to be shifting to her apartment. When she did, he didn't take it very well.

'Don't tell me you are serious! You will stay with a guy in the same apartment and you think I will be okay with it?' Sid shouted.

She looked around to check if somebody could hear their conversation. Thankfully, there was not a person in sight.

'I am not asking for your permission. I am simply informing you. And if you don't trust me, you can just go to hell. I don't care. I am not your slave and I won't dance to your tune. Be a man, don't be so insecure. You have to accept me the way I am. I don't like restrictions and until date I have lived life my way. No one can stop me from doing that. Not even you.'

'Who do you think you are? If you girls are so desperate, I can give you the fun you want. Why do you want a stranger in your house?'

The mention of her friends angered Ahana even more. He had no business including them in their personal fight. Ahana couldn't take it any longer. She grabbed her bag and left in anger. Sid tried to stop her but she had made up her mind. No one, not even Sid, could step on her or her friends' dignity.

All relationships come with their fair share of fights. Sid stood there helplessly. He knew Ahana was not like other girls who would submit to a man's wishes. The only choice he had was to accept Ahana the way she was. There was nothing wrong in doing this. When you love someone, you accept the person with all their flaws. She was not betraying him in any way. Sid knew he had overreacted in aggression.

A man raising his voice can shock and threaten a woman, but a woman's silence can thoroughly shake the consciousness of a man, and Sid was completely shaken!

'Where are you? We have reached PVR,' said Malvika over the phone to Ahana. It was a Sunday and they had decided to watch a movie together.

'I will reach in five minutes. Just parking the car in the basement,' Ahana replied and disconnected.

Ahana was slightly disturbed by Sid's behaviour. Since they weren't serious about each other as yet, she didn't expect him to impinge on her freedom and decisions. Obviously, her life was her own and Sid's attitude reflected his insecurity more than care. That had actually hurt her more. Resolving not to think much about it, she set off to enjoy the evening with Malvika and Garima.

'That's my tee, you whore,' Ahana screamed as she reached the theatre and saw Malvika at the ticket counter wearing her T-shirt.

'I was getting late. I don't know why it takes my hair so damn long to dry. Then I didn't find anything good in my closet to wear for today. I was like, "Not this outfit. Nope, not this either. No. No. Hate this one. Yikes, why do I still own that one? No. Nope." Then Garima finally suggested that I raid your closet. And I was jealous. Why do you have a better wardrobe than me? Then I thought I should steal your Superman tee for the movie.'

'I just hate sharing my clothes.'

'Don't worry. You can wear my lingerie for the entire week,' Malvika added.

Garima couldn't control her laughter at the annoyed look on Ahana's face. There was nothing she could do now. All three of them went inside the theatre and took their seats. There was a guy sitting at the extreme left next to Ahana. The movie started and, after some time, Ahana could feel a hand caressing her bare back. She had come wearing a tube top. A few seconds later, she could feel another hand grazing her thigh. For a moment she thought it was Malvika but looking sideways she saw that Malvika was quietly watching the movie. She realized it was an unfamiliar touch when she felt the roughness of the hand. It frightened her for a second, but suddenly she turned towards his side and slapped the person hard enough to make him fall off his seat. As she got up, she kicked and stomped hard on his groin twice and ran, signalling for Malvika and Garima to come with her. From the back door, all three of them made a quick getaway and ran until they reached the elevator. Once in, Garima asked her what had happened.

'Someone tried to play cricket with me and I played badminton with him.'

'What?'

'Ya. This man sitting next to me tried to grope my boobs in the darkness and I smashed his cock and ran out. And anyway the movie was fucking irritating.'

Both Malvika and Garima broke out into giggles. 'You're such a badass,' they exclaimed in unison.

Ahana and Malvika were completely insane and Garima too enjoyed their company. She had finally started enjoying life away from home, the life she had wished for. Now that she had one hell of a gang, she never wanted to go back home.

'I salute your attitude!' Garima exclaimed, showing the middle finger to Ahana.

'Some people flirt with danger; I take it on a date and make it pay.' Ahana winked.

They sped homewards after that.

'Tonight I am going to promise myself that I won't fall anywhere,' Malvika declared.

'I'm already looking forward to having a hangover tomorrow,' Ahana added.

'Hopefully we will take many pictures tonight. Because I am sure Malvika doesn't want to waste this outfit,' Garima teased.

'I feel like changing my outfit ten more times.'

'Don't worry, you will be done with this feeling once you finish the first half of the vodka and then convince yourself that this is the greatest outfit you've ever worn,' Ahana said in amusement. Their chatter and teasing continued until they got home and opened a vodka bottle. Garima opened up a bottle of Coke and poured it into a glass.

'Cheers,' they all said in chorus as they lifted their glasses.

Ahana and Malvika sipped their vodka while Garima sipped on her cold drink. Within an hour the vodka was over and they opened another bottle. Both of them felt tipsy but continued drinking. When vodka goes in, your consciousness goes out! Ahana and Malvika clicked a selfie and uploaded it on Instagram.

'You should drink responsibly,' Garima suggested, looking at them struggling to sit properly.

'I will drink responsibly when there is a brand of vodka named Responsibly,' Ahana joked.

Malvika laughed and said, 'This vodka tastes a lot like I'm-not-going-to-work-tomorrow.'

'You both are crazy.' Garima smiled.

'Even you should try drinking this. Vodka is made of potatoes. Potatoes are vegetables which are good for you.' Ahana smiled.

Garima ignored her offer and glanced at Malvika who was looking deep into her mobile screen.

'What are you looking at so seriously? Porn?' Garima asked.

'No. I am actually thinking about this hot guy who keeps "liking" my Instagram pictures but never really texts me.'

'Awww. You should start liking his pictures, then probably he will,' Garima suggested.

Ahana came up with an idea. 'Why don't we play a prank by calling random people and harassing them?'

'They will get our numbers. It's risky,' Garima warned her.

'No. They won't. We will call using VOIP that will let us make calls via the computer without revealing our number. No one will ever get to know.' Ahana winked.

'Superb. It will be fun,' Malvika chimed in.

They dialled a random number. It was three in the morning.

'Hello,' the person on the other end said in a sleepy voice.

'Can I talk to Ramesh?' Ahana asked and chuckled.

'Wrong number, madam.'

'Then can I talk to Suresh?' she asked again, this time more seriously.

'Who do you want to talk with?' he asked in a furious tone.

'Any one. Ramesh or Suresh. I don't mind either,' Malvika added.

'Who are you? Have you gone nuts? It's three in the morning!'

'Achha woh chodiye, tell me one thing. Bachhe kaise paida hote hai? We are innocent and don't know how kids are born. Can you tell us?'

The person disconnected the call and all three of them rolled on the floor laughing. They weren't done yet. They dialled another number. Again a guy picked up in a sleepy tone.

'You sexy hunk, tell me one thing. Do you know how kids are born?'

This time the guy didn't disconnect the call. Instead the pervert actually started explaining things to them.

'First, you have to get naked with me, then I will lick you everywhere and then I will insert—' he continued.

This time the girls disconnected the call and the prank had them in splits.

'This guy's hand will hurt thinking about us.' Ahana laughed.

They had a great time together, cracking hilarious jokes and playing pranks the entire night. Some people just disconnected the call while some took the joke sportingly and played along. There were some who even threatened to inform the police but it was immensely funny, all in all.

With time, their bonding had grown strong. When it comes to friends, it's not quantity but quality that matters. Though it was just the three of them, Ahana, Malvika and Garima had become thick friends and along with studying, they were living their life to the fullest. Soon their girlie paradise would need to make space for a guy.

Roomies

I'm sorry but you never encouraged me and you weren't there to tell me there's nothing to fear.
But you should have been there.
I'm sorry but you weren't the one to teach me to ride a bike.
But you should have been there.
I'm sorry but you never held me tight when I lacked strength.
But you should have been there.
I'm sorry you weren't the one to hold me when I cried.
But you should have been there.
I'm sorry to say that you will always be my father, but you will never be my dad!

Varun wrote the poem on a piece of paper, then crumpled the sheet and threw it in the bin. It was well past midnight.

Suddenly the doorbell rang. He knew all too well who it would be. His father had again come home in a drunken state. He helped his father in and put him to bed, holding his hand for a minute. He wanted to feel the loving touch of his father, something that he had never experienced in all these years. All that he could associate with his father's touch was his rage and violence. He had decided to speak to his dad in the morning about taking admission in Mumbai University. After mustering up some courage, Varun made up his mind. He was going to talk to his father the next morning. If he could convince him of his plan then it was fine, if not, he would run away to Mumbai. Either way Varun refused to stifle his dreams.

With so many thoughts running through the mind, he never realized when the clock struck 6 a.m. Though it was still early, his dad never allowed him to sleep beyond that hour. An army rule imposed on him even at home which frustrated him completely. But today he was going to speak his mind and express the feelings that had lain suppressed in his heart for ages. Generally a son is not very comfortable talking to his dad unless the discussion is about a cricket match or something casual. Today was slightly different.

Varun approached his father when he saw him sitting on the sofa reading a newspaper in the living room and chugging whisky from a glass.

'Dad, I want to discuss something with you,' Varun said politely as he sat on the chair in front of his father.

'What is it? I hope it's not about you doing some petty business in the future and spoiling your future by doing a BSc,' his dad said in a strict tone.

Before the discussion could even start, Varun's dad had passed the verdict. It was a strict no, and it made Varun furious.

'But why, Dad? What's your problem? It's my life and it's my choice of career,' he shouted.

'If you have to stay here in my house, it's not your choice. You have to make me proud by joining the army. Are we clear?' his dad said in anger, throwing down the newspaper.

'I don't want to be in the army. Army people are losers. Yes, they have respect in the outer world but at a personal level, they are real losers. They live a lonely life and when they realize that they have done nothing their entire lives, they start becoming violent with their families, they start placing restrictions and giving orders. Do you think we are your slaves? I wish Mom were alive today. She would have never let this happen. Even when my mom was dying, you preferred to stay away from home. Why? Because you had other useless duties to fulfil. My mother died in pain. She needed you. We needed you. Where were you at that time? Where were you when I was looking for a support system?

You preferred drinking over spending time with me or my mother! You always wanted us to live our lives your way. That's a dictatorship. I am not going to accept it. You are a killer.'

Varun's dad stood up and threw his glass of whisky to the floor. The broken glass was symbolic of the broken father-and-son relationship.

'What did you say? Army people are lonely? We sacrifice our lives so that billions of people in this country can breathe safely. We are the hope of countless families who enjoy festivals because we are fighting at the border. And you say that we are losers?' He screamed as loudly as he could.

'I don't care. Why should I bother? You might have lived your life for billions of people but my mother died alone. For my entire teenage life, I have lived alone. My friends were scared to come home due to your violent behaviour. You might have been the hope for countless families as they celebrated but we never enjoyed a festival together. Never ever! Do you have any justification for that?'

'I am not an emotional fool. Duty comes first for an army person and I did justice to my duty. Your mom had cancer and her death was on the cards irrespective of my being in the army or not. She died of cancer, it was not my mistake. Do you get that? All this rubbish that you say just goes to show how immature you are. I am going to teach you better. I am going to teach you a lesson even if it kills you.'

He took the belt that lay on the desk and started lashing Varun with it. Varun took the blows without even blinking an eye.

The lashing continued for some time. His father kept abusing him and Varun kept bearing it without saying a word. 'You son of a bitch, how dare you call me lonely and a loser? I am the one who provides you money and—' But when his father said 'son of a bitch', something happened to Varun. He caught hold of the belt with his hand and threw it away. Then, pushing his father back, he retaliated with a slap. 'How dare you abuse my mother?'

For a moment both of them stood there silently, without moving an inch. Varun had not slapped his father, he had slapped a man who was abusing his mother, who couldn't understand his son or his feelings, a man who could neither be a good father nor the head of his family, a drunkard who would violently beat up his son. For years now, Varun had held a grudge against his dad and he could never forgive him for neglecting him during his childhood.

Varun went inside his room and locked himself. Tears were streaming down his cheeks thinking of what had happened. He was human, and his emotions had given way to a volcanic eruption.

The very same day Varun booked his train ticket to Mumbai and as soon as his dad went for an evening walk, Varun packed his bags and everything that he would need during his stay. He had no option other than to run away. Before leaving, he put in his bag a photo frame with his mom's picture as he considered her his good luck charm. She was the one and only inspiration in his life. The only things left to take were his school certificates and some cash. He found the keys to his dad's locker in the dressing table. After packing all his necessary documents and picking up some cash, he wrote a harsh goodbye note for his father and placed it on the dressing table. Then he picked up his baggage and left, without once caring to turn back.

When Varun's dad returned, he saw the goodbye note Varun had left for him. Though he knew his son didn't like him very much, his departure was still a big shock to him. For a split second, he was blinded by complete darkness. He sat on the chair reaching out for the water bottle and reread the last line of the letter. *Please do not search for me if you are a real man. Live with it and be strong. After all, you are an army man!*

Varun's dad was shattered from within. He was his father, after all. The question that loomed large over his head was whether he should look for Varun or and give up on him.

Twenty hours later, Varun stepped on Mumbai soil, a city where he would build his dreams.

Varun called Ahana upon arrival and informed her that he was taking a cab to her house and would be reaching in an hour. Ahana shared the news with Malvika and Garima.

In one decisive moment, Varun's life had changed forever. Within a few days, Varun not only got admission to the college he had applied to, but also made friends with the other two flatmates—Malvika and Garima. A relationship is not dependent on the length of the time you have spent together; it's dependent on the foundation you have built together.

Varun was slightly more comfortable with Malvika than Garima and loved spending time with her, and Malvika too loved his company. As days passed, he started looking for a part-time job to pay for his monthly expenses. The cash he had brought with him was slowly running out. Though Ahana persuaded him to borrow some cash from her, he didn't want to be an added liability on her as it went against his own principles. She had helped him a lot with the accommodation already. Gradually they had become the secret ingredients to each other's happiness. Eventually he got a job at a café near the apartment.

All of them had their share of troubles and sorrows. Garima couldn't forget her past; it was like a splinter stuck in her heart forever. The one person that Varun couldn't forgive ever was his dad. Even though Ahana's dad wasn't as abusive, he still was indifferent towards her and that saddened her. But all of them had their dreams to chase and were passionate about them. Ahana wanted to be one of the country's top fashion designers, Malvika wanted to start her own dental practice, whereas Varun wanted to be an entrepreneur. Garima meanwhile just wanted to live a happy, independent life, the kind that had eluded her so far.

It's all in the moment, as they say, but it is important that the moment clicks. For these four, the moment had not only clicked but had framed a picture-perfect image.

Varun had just come home from college and was about to go for a bath when his phone rang. It was his dad. He picked up the call.

'How are you? And where are you?' his dad asked.

'Mind your own business,' Varun said.

'Why do you always behave like this and make me angry?' his dad replied.

'I do not want to talk you, so please stop calling me. Why do you care? Just get lost,' Varun screamed.

Malvika came into the room running. There was no one at home apart from the two of them. Ahana and Garima had left for college. Malvika had stayed back to prepare for an upcoming test.

'What happened?' she questioned; giving him a puzzled look.

'Nothing. It was my dad's call.'

Malvika asked him whether he was always as rude to his dad as he was now. Varun nodded and told her the reason for his anger. He told her how his dad used to beat him even for the slightest mistake and used to abuse him every day. While narrating the entire story, he got extremely emotional. He confessed that he missed his parents' involvement during his adolescent years. Malvika held his hand to convey that she understood how he felt. Varun felt a sense of security, the kind that he had missed his entire life, as Malvika sat there listening to him. 'Whatever it may be, he is your dad and I'm sure he loves you too,' Malvika whispered.

Varun got up but Malvika caught hold of his hand and pulled him back.

'Never judge someone without knowing the reason behind their behaviour. After your mom passed away, your dad must have felt lonely as well. Probably that's the reason he drinks so much. Did you ever try consoling him, telling him that you were going to be his strength? You could have shared whatever he felt. You could have tried being a friend rather than a son. You could have broken the ice, extending conversations beyond sports and news. Did you ever try this with him?'

All Varun could say in answer was a faint 'No'. He was dumbstruck. No one had ever explained things to him the way she did and he felt a deep connection with her in that moment. The best conversations occur when people talk with their eyes. Both Varun and Malvika were silent for a few seconds, just looking at each other.

Varun wanted to hug Malvika for trying to explain the situation but he knew it was too early for them to share a hug.

'Would you like to have some coffee?' Malvika said, breaking the awkward silence.

'Yes, but only if something's going to happen over that cup of coffee,' Varun flirted.

Malvika just smiled and went into the kitchen. Varun had a shower and changed into his boxers. Giving him a cup of coffee, Malvika went into her room. She was suddenly not feeling too well. Varun was contemplating whether to enter her room or not. It was not as if he had never walked into her room but today there was no one at home. He finished his coffee and knocked on her door.

'Come in,' said Malvika, still lying on her bed.

'Hey. Are you fine? You look dull.'

'You mean that I don't look beautiful?' Malvika teased him.

'Of course you do, you are beautiful. There is something charming about you that can awaken even a dead soul. And it's not just your outer beauty, it's your qualities as a friend. The way you explained things so beautifully to me, it was incredible. Your parents are very lucky to have a daughter like you.'

Varun realized that he had praised her a little more than he should have. But it was apparent now that he liked her, so why shouldn't he praise her? The best way to impress a girl is to praise her for her qualities and not just her outwardly beauty. Malvika blushed and they talked for a couple of minutes more before Varun realized that he was still standing at the door.

'Can I enter your room? Or is entry for boys banned?' asked Varun.

'Oh, I'm so sorry! I didn't realize you were standing all this while. Please come in,' Malvika replied, going red in the face again.

He settled himself on her bed and they continued to talk about various topics including professors, sexy girls, hot guys, celebrities, sex and relationships. He felt the urge to touch her, not physically but to touch her heart and soul, to discover the things that she kept locked within, to be one with her thoughts. He wanted to understand her as a person. He felt it was too early and he didn't want to sound desperate. However, love is love and you don't decide whom you fall in love with or when you fall for them. Somewhere, somehow, in some nook of his heart, he knew that he had fallen for Malvika.

Happy Hours of Singlehood

It was a sunny afternoon and Varun was working his shift at the café. Being a weekend, there was a huge rush at the café and while waiting on one of the tables, Varun's belt broke. He had to walk back with both his hands holding on to the pants so that they didn't slide down. He called Garima and told her to rush to the café with another belt from his closet.

For the next half an hour Varun didn't wait on any tables as it was impossible for him to hold the dishes in one hand and his pants with the other. A slight mistake would have cost him either a deduction from his salary or the embarrassment of a lifetime. He knew he would be red in the face if his pants came down in front of so many people, including a good number of girls. He just prayed for Garima to reach as soon as possible.

I am one of those rare men who pray that his pants don't slip off so that I can resume work while a majority of men pray that someone will pull their pants down and start working,' he thought to himself as he waited in a corner of the café kitchen. His colleagues were trying hard not to laugh while his manager was getting really furious. Luckily for him, Garima reached the place just before the manager could fire him and handed over his belt.

'You are a saviour. Thank God. I was going to lose all my dignity otherwise,' said Varun, breathing a sigh of relief.

'I just hope this does not repeat itself. If it does, your only hope of survival would be your manager. That too if he is gay.' Garima laughed.

Garima was about to leave as Varun's manager was already ranting about him wasting time. That's when she saw something that astounded her. Ahana's boyfriend Sid was getting cosy on the corner couch with some other girl. They were so close that even a blind person could have sensed what was going on between the two.

'What happened?' Varun asked, noticing her reaction.

'That is . . . Sid . . . Ahana's boyfriend . . . What is he doing here with . . .' Garima stammered.

Varun watched him closely and tried to recollect the picture Ahana had shown him once.

'Are you sure? I mean I have never seen him personally. She just showed me a picture once.'

'Yes, I am.'

Garima took her mobile from her bag and discreetly clicked pictures and took a video of Sid cosying up to the girl so that she could show them to Ahana. Else Ahana might not have believed her word. Even if she did, Sid wouldn't have accepted it.

'This guy comes here almost every day. Mostly in the afternoon,' Varun added, giving Garima a surprised look.

Garima just glanced at him but didn't utter a word. After clicking enough pictures and videos she went back to the apartment where she found Ahana filing her nails. Garima had no clue how to tell her that her boyfriend was two-timing her. The relationship that Ahana had considered just a passing affair had never really existed for Sid. Garima sat next to her and with all the courage she could muster, she blurted out the truth.

'Sid is double-dating. He is sleeping around with another girl.'

Ahana was shocked and didn't know whether to believe her or not. She turned towards Garima and was about to pounce on her when Garima showed her the pictures on her mobile phone. Ahana stood there speechlessly. Though she always put up a brave front, now a tear rolled down her cheek. Every single teardrop had memories attached to it. Good or bad but memories nevertheless! In a fraction of a moment, everything flashed before her eyes. The fact that

Sid loved someone else didn't hurt her much but she was completely against two-timing a person.

She wanted to call him the moment she saw all the photographs and videos but Garima stopped her, saying, 'Don't call him now. That will alert him. Varun told me he comes to the café every day. Varun didn't know he was your boyfriend since he had seen him just once in a picture you had showed him. But instead of calling him now, we should catch him red-handed in the café tomorrow.'

Ahana found her argument sensible and decided to play along to expose Sid in front of a huge group of people.

'The only thing he will have in his mouth apart from his dick will be my name now. Treat me like a princess; I'll treat you like a prince. Treat me like a game; I'll show you how it's played,' Ahana exclaimed.

A person who prefers to have an affair outside of a relationship always forgets that not every open eye is seeing, and not every closed eye is sleeping. Sid would have thought that he could play around and Ahana would never come to know, but he had been spotted. Usually lies don't end relationships. The truth does. Sid had probably been lying for a long time but now when the truth was out, Ahana decided to put an end to their relationship.

The next morning Ahana felt so different from the person she usually was. She felt heartless. There had been fights before with Sid but now she was going to end it once and for all. She couldn't respect him any more. She wanted him to pay the price for trying to fool her, so that he would be afraid to treat anyone else in a similar manner. The whole thing had taught her a valuable lesson—you can't know the complete truth about a person, no matter how familiar you are with them.

Ahana and Garima went to the café in the afternoon. The entire way, Garima counselled her to keep a check on her aggression. But Ahana had made up her mind to kick his balls as hard as she could. She wanted to make him realize that cheating on women was not a cool idea. When it came to her dignity and pride, she could completely ruin a person for hurting her.

Varun had informed them beforehand that Sid was sitting inside with the same girl.

'You can come inside but please see to it that you don't break the furniture,' Varun teased, escorting them in from the back door.

Furious, Ahana stormed into the café. Everyone turned around to look at her, including Sid. He anxiously stood up as soon as he saw Ahana staring down at him.

'It's over,' Ahana screamed as loudly as possible.

For a split second, Sid was embarrassed as all the people in the café were looking at them. The other girl with him looked confused. Ahana went closer to him and said, 'Don't be so surprised. Yes, I have caught you red-handed but I was already aware of your cheap fucking trick. Thanks to Garima, I know the truth now. She showed me pictures and clips of you getting cosy with this girl. I wouldn't have known if Garima had not come to the café yesterday. You fucking son of a whore, your dick should be chopped off and you should be made to run naked all over the street. Maybe that will teach you a lesson or two. You should know what it's like to be cheated on.'

'You are not even giving me a chance to speak,' Sid said, his face red with shame.

'You are such an asshole!'

Ahana pulled his cheeks mockingly and kicked him in the groin. The kick was so painful that he fell on the couch holding his balls. But more than the physical pain, it was the embarrassment that hurt Sid. Varun stood there watching the entire scene. With Ahana at the centre of things, there was no need for him to interfere. She was totally capable of dealing with the situation herself. With her uncontrollable aggression, she was handling everything just fine.

Sid left the café in complete humiliation. He had not expected something like this to happen! One realizes the worth of what they have only when they lose it. This was true for Sid as well. He was heartbroken.

A few hours had passed when Ahana received a message from him.

I know there are a lot of things I did and I haven't thought long enough before doing them. I have lied to you so many times without thinking that it's you I really care about and I never thought I would lose you. I could trade my life just to tell you one last time that though I committed mistakes, even you were not always right. But I know you have moved on, your expressions said so. I took you for granted. But how could you go away so easily? How can you be such a bitch without even thinking twice? Your company mattered at some point in time. But now it doesn't. Why should it matter when it doesn't matter to you? Get lost and don't forget that you once used to sleep naked with me on my bed. Fuck off.

Sid was going through extreme mood swings. One second he wanted Ahana back in his life and the next second he didn't since she had been the one to call it off so easily. Did she ever care about him at all? Because of that frustration, gradually the 'love' in the message turned to 'hate'. However, Ahana didn't bother replying as she was not a sob queen from Bollywood—helpless, weak and silly over lost love. She was strong mentally and emotionally and was independent enough to handle her life her way. When her dad's behaviour didn't affect her emotionally, how could Sid's? She wouldn't have cared had Sid broken up first and then dated someone. But he preferred to cheat on her which annoyed her no end. When you let someone into your life full-time and they only let you in part-time, it's time to move on.

When Garima and Ahana came back to their room, Malvika had already ordered pizza for them to celebrate Ahana's singlehood.

'Finally you are single and now you can upload as many seductive selfies as you want on Instagram and even check in more frequently on Facebook. You don't have to monitor your boyfriend's Facebook to see if his ex is liking his photos or commenting on them. Now your phone bills will be reduced to half and you will get sound sleep every night. You don't have to worry thinking about which café to go to during weekends nor will you be forced to watch action movies. You can just lock yourself up in your pyjamas and stay in bed. Your time will be all yours and when birthdays and Valentine's Day roll around, you don't need to buy dozens of gifts. You'll save thousands of rupees by staying single. Just think of all that you can do with that money. Lots of vodka shots and pizzas. You can actually flirt around town and even upload photos with your male friends more frequently. And lastly, you don't have to wax during winters as under layers of clothes. No immature guy is going to see your skin and shriek upon spotting a bit of hair.'

Malvika ran out of breath and paused for a second, then added, 'I think you should throw a break-up party tonight.'

Ahana was laughing at whatever she said and hugged her. She even agreed to throw a party once Varun got back from the café. She couldn't be angry with her friends who had made such an elaborate effort to make her smile and stood by her selflessly. All four of them were more than a family now.

The final process of maturity is realizing that you can't be angry at the world because of your experience with a few stupid, selfish people! When people start acting like the split ends in your hair, cut them off without warning before they cause more damage.

'Gorgeous!' Ahana exclaimed, looking at Malvika.

Malvika had put on a knee-length skirt and a black halter-neck top. Her eyeliner and glossy lips made her charming face shine a little more than usual. Varun was dumbstruck looking at her.

'I think I'm in love.' Varun winked.

'Oh shut up. Let's move. Are we heading to the same place that I suggested?' Malvika added.

'Yes. Palladium Mall in Lower Parel.'

'Where is Garima?' Varun asked.

'I am here,' she replied, coming out from the bedroom.

Everyone was speechless looking at Garima. For the first time since they had all moved in, Garima was wearing a dress. It was a full-length one-piece pink dress with a similar colour headband. She looked really cute in it. Everyone hugged her and Malvika could feel her eyes dampening with tears. She had always wanted Garima to destroy her past demons and enjoy her life to the fullest. Though she was still far from being absolutely comfortable in the company of outsiders, she was getting there with time. She was making an attempt to mix and be more social, trying to overcome the bitterness.

'Wow. Never knew you could actually make someone go weak with just one look at you,' Ahana said, hugging Garima. Then she said excitedly, 'Okay guys, how about going wild tonight?'

'Now what?'

'How about using a penis straw tonight at the party?' Ahana winked.

Everyone glanced at each other with quizzical expressions on their faces. Ahana went inside and brought a couple of straws that were shaped like penises. She had ordered them online a few months ago just for fun.

'All you have to do is suck it. Oops, I mean suck on the straw and drink your beer.' Ahana gave a demo which embarrassed Varun and Garima but made Malvika laugh out loud.

'It's tacky. Don't take it along with you, please,' said Garima.

'Some think it's tacky; I think it's funny. When we used it the last time, the waiter almost died of shock. It's a cute way to have a little fun at the party.'

'Are you freaking serious?' asked Varun.

Ahana was not in the mood to listen to reason and carried them with her.

When they reached the lounge, the manager announced that there was a 'Pi until you pee' offer on, which was similar to a beer bladder burst where you are allowed to drink free of cost until you pee.

Malvika and Ahana decided to participate in the contest. Varun had to drive Ahana's car back so he refrained from drinking too much.

'Ready, girl?' Ahana asked Malvika to which she nodded.

Within an hour, both the girls had already gulped down four glasses of draught beer. Ahana felt a little dizzy and just to check her level of drunkenness, she tried walking back and forth in the bar. She was swaying while walking and the situation was pretty fucked up. Malvika decided to stop as she wanted to go to the loo.

'You loser, you are going to pee after just four drinks. You should learn self-control. It helps during sex too,' Ahana screamed.

Varun had no clue how to respond to this. Four more drinks and that was it. She had reached her threshold. Her bladder wasn't bursting but she was completely out of her senses.

Ahana was so high that she was smiling and waving at every guy she saw in the bar. No matter what people said, she was just screaming, 'I am not high; I am just pretending to be.'

Suddenly Varun spotted a college friend and waved at him. He caught Ahana's attention and she went after him, asking him to join them. The guy was shit-scared and ran away.

'I am in the mood. I need a guy . . . I am in the mood.' She was screaming as they made their way to the car.

Varun was worried now as the situation was getting worse. Garima had handled Malvika but it was difficult to handle Ahana. Somehow they both made her sit in the car and Varun started driving.

'I am not going to allow them to drink so much from now on,' Garima stated, looking at Varun in the rear-view mirror.

'I was shit-scared,' confessed Varun.

Ahana kept talking about stupid things until Varun screamed at her to let him drive.

'I need to pee,' she screamed and started tapping her feet. Varun was seriously scared now.

'Susu karni hai,' she screamed out loud.

Small smiles crossed Varun's and Garima's faces. Varun stopped at a lounge on the way and decided to take her in so that she could use the washroom. Malvika was asleep and thus Garima waited in the car while Varun accompanied Ahana to the washroom. She wore an expression of relief on her face once she came out after nearly five minutes. While leaving, a random guy showed up and asked Varun, 'Is she your girlfriend?'

Varun smiled and said, 'No.'

'Mind if I take her along for a while?' he asked and made his first move by grabbing Ahana's hand.

Varun was slightly scared as they started interacting.

'Are you an IITian?' Ahana asked in a tipsy voice.

He almost laughed and said yes.

'No doubt. All IITians are bloody despos,' Varun added.

Ahana bent towards him and gave him a tiny peck on his cheek. There was something really sweet about him even though he was a complete nerd.

He laughed and said that was not what he was expecting.

'You can now enjoy the next four years of IIT. Anyway, it sucks big time.'

Ahana laughed and bid him goodbye.

Ahana was terrifying and strange and beautiful. But her roommates loved her completely. Garima was slowly opening up and though she was reserved, all three of them cared for her a lot. Malvika lived for the moment and the one thing that everyone liked about her was that she was very frank. Varun was very understanding and knew how to handle women, which made him a favourite with the three girls. The moment they stepped into each other's lives was the moment their lives truly began!

Dear Life, You Suck!

'Have you informed Malvika that I am coming along with you?' Ahana asked Garima.

'Yes, I told her we will be reaching in some time,' Garima replied as she shuffled the radio channels in the car.

Ahana was giving Garima a ride to college since she had her oral exams and didn't want to take public transport. Ahana had decided to drop her off and then spend some time with Varun on campus and come back to the apartment together with everyone. She didn't have any important assignments on that day so it was not a big thing for her to miss college. Malvika's batch had an exam in the morning while Garima's was in the afternoon.

'You can park the car there,' Garima said, guiding her as she was new to their campus.

'Don't worry, darling. I will park the car and come. You carry on.' Ahana smiled.

Garima got off and started walking towards the college building which was not very far from the parking lot. Midway, she saw the group that liked to tease her by calling her a virgin and also playing pranks on her. She would try not to pay them attention but they did make her furious sometimes. But she knew it was best to ignore them to avoid creating a scene in college. This time too as she walked past them, they started passing lewd comments.

'Here comes the virgin queen. Virginity is the lack of opportunity,' said one of the girls in the group.

'If you want, I can be the opportunity and ensure that you lose your virginity,' said a guy.

'She is saving it for her husband, it seems,' laughed another girl.

'Can I be your husband for a night?' asked another boy.

'Such a loser you are. You don't know how to enjoy life. Sex is for fun and we live in modern times. There's nothing wrong with having some fun, is there?' said a girl who held a cigarette in her hand.

The comments kept pouring in and this time she couldn't stop herself from reacting.

'That's it! What's wrong with you guys? It's your choice if you want to sleep around and fuck the whole day. I simply opt out of this "fun". Who are you to comment on my personal life and talk shit? Look at yourself first and then open your lousy mouths, you fuckers,' Garima said furiously.

'Oh ho . . . so you can use cuss words too? Then it won't be that difficult for you. You can use it to motivate your boyfriend so that he can go hard on you,' one of the girls shouted.

By this time Ahana had parked the car and was making her way in and she heard their conversation. When the gang saw Ahana approach the group, one of the girls commented, 'Do you also fall in the same group of lonely virgins?'

Ahana reacted strongly. 'I am a woman who is far more modern than you think you are and far more independent than your mom. If your dad had used a condom that night, he would have saved the planet from scumbag motherfuckers like you. You think losing your virginity is cool? And you, you guys, haven't your mothers taught you to keep your dicks inside your pants? Teri maa ki . . . Don't teach your mother a lesson in virginity, you jerk. And the girls in the group—have you no shame?'

One of the guys tried to hit Ahana but Garima broke in, saying, 'I dare you. I will kick you so hard that you will never walk erect. Stay away. Don't think of every silent girl as weak. If they decide to hit back, you will realize that guys cry louder than women. Be real men who respect women instead of threatening them and bullying them with physical force.'

Her words had silenced the entire group. They bowed their heads in shame. Sometimes people forget other people's feelings. Ahana and Garima had taught them a valuable lesson and they would think twice before teasing another girl.

'Well done, my girl.' Ahana patted her.

Garima smiled and called Malvika to ask her whereabouts. She was sitting alone in the canteen in a low mood. Ahana and Garima came and sat near her and asked her the reason for her unhappiness. She told them her parents were insisting she get married as soon as she graduated.

'They say the right age for a girl to get married is twenty-three. I mean, where on earth is it written that if I cross twenty-three I can't stay single? Who made such creepy rules?'

'You still have a long way to go, darling,' Ahana consoled her.

'Yes I know, but all they have to talk about is marriage. I was just talking to them about general things and was telling them how the first semester will soon be over and they started saying how they wanted me to graduate soon and get married to the perfect guy. Spare me,' Malvika said in disgust.

'I have a better option. Once you are done with graduation, take admission to a postgraduate course. Most people who opt for PG do it to postpone their inevitable marriage.' Garima laughed.

'It's not a joke. Doing this graduation is worse than a *Roadies* task and you are talking about postgraduation. They keep pestering me to get married and they talk about it all the time . . . I mean ALL the time. I will stop calling them from now on. If we don't have the right to even choose our partner and are supposed to get married as soon as we graduate, then why the hell do we bother to study so much when we can't even enjoy our life with our money and opportunities? I so hate this.'

'Are you planning to join a women's empowerment group?' Varun said, tapping her back, upon hearing her strong views against marriage.

Everyone laughed and Varun took his seat beside them.

'By the way, you have all the right to choose a guy you want.' Varun winked.

Malvika went red in the face and Ahana caught her blushing. Ahana knew that Varun and Malvika secretly had a crush on each other and were trying their best to hide it from each other and the group.

'Don't waste your time staring at the person you're in love with. Get up and go tell them you're in love with them before it's too late and they're gone,' she stated.

Garima giggled and they high-fived. She had understood what Ahana was trying to say. Varun and Malvika avoided looking at each other. Just then Varun got a call from his dad that changed his mood completely. He picked up the call and left the table. Garima too left for her oral exams. Malvika and Ahana chit-chatted for some time until Varun returned. His frustration was visible on his face.

'What is it between you and your dad that always makes you angry?' Ahana had to ask.

'It's okay. Don't worry. Just remember what I told you.' Malvika held his hand.

'OMG! She knows and I still don't. Wow Varun, you are too fast. You never told me.'

She tried to make him smile but he sat there expressionless. When Malvika left to attend her lecture, Varun told her everything. He cried in front of her as she was his most trustworthy friend.

'I needed him in the good and bad times. But all he ever did was to shout at me and abuse me. I sometimes feel like I am not even his son. How can a father be so cruel?' he sobbed.

Ahana heard him out patiently without passing any judgement. Varun added, 'I just wish he would come here running to support me. I wish he would talk to me about my plans and aspirations.'

'I understand,' Ahana replied.

Hearing Varun's story Ahana started reflecting on her own relationship with her father. But that's how life is. If we get everything we desire, we would never realize the importance of striving for it. Ups and downs are necessary in life. Depression gets to us and makes us shut ourselves away from the world. It makes us lock ourselves in when the people outside are just waiting for us to open up and smile at them. Ahana somewhere missed the presence of her dad in her happiness; Garima was taunted for her innocence by some stupid college group; Malvika was being pressurized to get married as soon as she completed her graduation though she had just joined college; Varun realized that he needed his father to be around him even though his father didn't think of him the same way.

All four of them were lost in their own thoughts on their way back home in Ahana's car. Ahana saw Garima and Malvika in the rear-view mirror; they looked really sad.

'Why don't we plan a road trip? A random one. We all have our own sorrows but it doesn't mean we should just cry over them and forget to enjoy life. Forget whatever happened today and let's just enjoy. Let's celebrate our friendship and togetherness. We are all family, after all,' she suggested.

No one reacted for a few seconds but the idea enthralled everyone.

'Sounds exciting. We will turn our GPS off and just drive wherever the road takes us. It will be a lot of fun. We can start tonight,' said Varun, almost jumping in excitement.

A few years ago there was no GPS. Sometimes we get lost and find better places than we'd initially planned. All of them had decided to celebrate their togetherness on a random road trip, forgetting their sorrows. Sometimes the person you need the most, and rely on to support you, leaves you alone. Some people get depressed and end their lives, while some, like Ahana, Garima, Malvika and Varun, decide to deal with it and still find their moments of bliss!

Let's Get Lost…

College days are not for worrying about the world outside but for celebrating togetherness with your friends from whom you will probably separate as they walk on their own chosen path a few years later.

The four of them decided to go on their random road trip that night itself. The rules were simple. They would not use the GPS for navigation to see if they were on the right track. No mobile phones and debit cards. No connection with the outside world. Phones switched off and life switched on. The destination didn't matter to them as they wanted to make their journey memorable. They wanted it to be an adventurous trip, one they would remember for a long time to come. It was decided that Ahana would drive as she was a stranger to Mumbai roads and would not know the right way, which was exactly the purpose of the journey, unlike Malvika who was a born Mumbaikar. Before the start of the journey, they had withdrawn enough money from an ATM in case they needed it for an emergency along the way. 'I hope you have checked everything?' Varun asked as he shoved the money into his wallet.

'Yes,' Garima replied, getting into the car.

'Has everyone put their phones in their bags? We are not going to use them, so tuck them away in your bags safely,' Varun stated.

'Obviously, we will keep them in a safe place. We live in a world where losing your phone is more scary than losing your virginity.' Ahana laughed.

They cruised along Palm Beach Road with music playing on full blast. Varun took out some hash from his pocket and rolled a joint. After taking a few drags, he passed the joint to Ahana. They were listening to 'Manali Trance' from the movie *Shaukeens*. Like Lisa Haydon, Ahana was swaying to the number and driving the car at full speed.

As they neared the end of Palm Beach, they saw a guy trying to hitch a ride. Ahana slowed the car so they could take a better look at him. 'I think we should help him. He looks decent enough,' Malvika said.

'It's not safe to be picking up strangers. Let's move on,' Varun added.

But Ahana didn't listen to him and stopped the car. Slowly she lowered the window and asked the guy where he wanted to go.

'Can you please drop me until Mankhurd if you are going the same way? I've been looking for transport for the last hour,' the guy said in an effeminate voice.

'Sure,' Ahana declared.

The guy came and sat next to Varun who had to scoot to the middle to make room for him. Malvika was seated to Varun's right. Garima was sitting in front and had no problem with a stranger sitting in the car. Ahana pressed the accelerator once again and turned left on the Sion–Panvel highway as directed by the unknown traveller. Just as Varun was dozing off, he sensed a hand grazing his thigh. Thinking it was Malvika, he let it continue for some time. But when he opened his eyes slightly, he got the shock of his life. It wasn't Malvika but the guy sitting next to him!

'Dude, what the fuck do you think you're doing?'

Ahana looked back to see what the commotion was about. Malvika couldn't stop laughing, looking at Varun's awkward situation.

'Ahana, stop the car. That's it. Take your hand away, you moron,' Varun screamed as the guy tried to touch him again.

Ahana and the girls were enjoying seeing Varun uncomfortable. Instead of stopping the car, Ahana encouraged the guy, saying Varun was gay and was looking for a boyfriend.

Spurred on by the girls' response, he tried to get hold of Varun's 'package', making Varun scream out in terror!

'Why are you screaming, handsome? Keep calm and enjoy yourself. This will be an experience of a lifetime for you,' the guy whispered in his ear in a seductive tone.

'Ahana, are you going to stop the car or should I jump out?' Varun screamed.

'Darling, we are on the bridge. If you jump out now, you'll fall straight into the river. I suggest you get out on flat ground once we cross the bridge,' joked Ahana.

'Why are you doing this?' asked Varun, turning to the guy.

'I love how your nipples are visible through your shirt. And the dragon in your pants—'

Before he could finish, Varun screamed, 'Fuck you, man. Spare me the horror. You are sexually harassing me.' The more he screamed, the more everyone laughed at his situation.

'What's your name, by the way?' Ahana asked, looking at the guy in the rear-view mirror.

'What's in a name? It's all down there. A person is recognized by his size and Varun, by that standard, is quite blessed . . . if you know what I mean,' the guy said in a seductive manner only to embarrass Varun more.

For the first time Varun felt that living with three girls was actually a lot safer than living with a guy who turned out to be gay. He felt helpless and wanted to bang his head on a wall somewhere while all the girls continued to make fun of him. Finally Ahana stopped the car and Varun pushed the guy out of the car.

'You people think this was funny? It felt like I was being raped. He even touched my privates!'

'Did he stroke you well?' Malvika winked.

'It's not funny at all. Shit. I almost wanted to . . . I want some beer. I want it right now. Enough of all this nonsense,' Varun screamed in frustration.

A man instantly knows when a seemingly nice guy is actually an asshole just as a woman instantly knows when a sweet woman is actually a bitch! He had sensed something wrong the very minute he saw the guy asking for a lift.

'What place is this? Malvika, do you know?' Ahana asked.

'How the fuck is that related to beer?' Varun screamed again.

'I am not too sure since it's dark, but I think we are somewhere in western Mumbai,' Malvika said, looking outside.

After driving for a few more kilometres, they were able to locate a wine and beer shop. Ahana stopped the car and told Varun to bring a few bottles of beer. Varun had placed his wallet in a bag placed below his seat. He bent down to fetch it and saw that the bag's zip was already open. He panicked and looked for the wallet but to no avail. The others asked him to search elsewhere in case he had dropped it somewhere in the car, but he was certain he had put it in the bag. Everyone told him to check once again but he found nothing. And then it dawned on him! The weirdo they had given a free ride to was not only a potential rapist but a thief as well who had robbed them of all their money and had fun at their expense.

'How did he know the wallet was in there?' Garima asked in shock.

'How am I supposed to know? I might have left the bag unzipped but I'm not too certain,' exclaimed Varun.

'How could you be so careless? We are totally fucked now,' Malvika squeaked at Varun.

None of them were carrying their ATM cards. They were now left with no money at all. The random trip had suddenly turned into their worst nightmare.

'Now how are we going to get cash? We don't have our cards either,' Malvika sobbed.

Ahana tried to lift the mood of the group by saying, 'Varun, chuck it. Why don't you just donate your sperm at one of the fertility centres nearby? We will get sufficient cash for it. A little charity won't harm you.'

'Dude, that's a nice idea. You want me to Google some sperm banks around here?' Malvika said in excitement.

'Just go for it. Be a man. Shake well and ring the bell.' Ahana winked.

'You girls are too much. Anyway, there's no need for it. I don't want to be the next Vicky Donor.'

'Not Vicky. Varun . . . Varun Donor.' Garima laughed.

Luckily, while rummaging through his pockets, Varun found a five-hundred-rupee note.

'That's all I have,' Varun proclaimed, showing the note to everyone.

'We can still get three bottles of vodka. And anyway, we have sufficient petrol in the car. The only concern is we won't be able to eat anything later. But that's fine . . . who wants to eat when we have enough to drink?' Ahana exclaimed.

Varun got out of the car and went to the wine shop. Ahana had parked the car right across from the shop, by the side of the highway. There was a huge crowd of men outside the shop trying to buy liquor. Varun tried to make his way to the centre and shouted out his order, but his screams went unheard. He was already frustrated with everything that had happened and this waiting business was getting on his nerves. He screamed once again but the counter boy responded angrily and told him to be patient as he was attending to other customers.

With no choice left, Varun stood in the corner. It was while waiting here that he saw beer crates piled up one over the other in the dark. Suddenly an idea struck him!

He glanced at the shop owner and the counter boy who were busy collecting cash and attending to customers. Varun looked around to see if anyone was watching but everyone was busy doing their own thing. In a fraction of a second, Varun picked up a crate of beer and ran faster than Milka Singh. The difference was that while Milka ran for the pride of the nation, Varun ran to save himself from the humiliation he would face if he were caught. Ahana saw Varun running towards them with the crate and immediately turned on the ignition.

By then the shopkeeper had seen him running and was hot on his heels.

'Ruk, teri maa ki. Ruk, saale,' he yelled at Varun as he ran behind him.

'Run . . . run . . . faster,' cheered Ahana.

Malvika opened the door and Varun jumped in. Ahana stepped on the accelerator even before they could shut the door of the car. Within a few minutes, they crossed Malad and took the route towards Mind Space, Malad. They spent the night near Madh Island where Malvika recounted a few horror stories about the place until they were scared stiff.

One should not wait for happy endings to come; one should create happy endings. Had they thought of a destination, they would not have enjoyed the journey as they did now. It had indeed turned out to be one hell of a road trip for them. They had managed to drink beer for free and had eaten some street food with the last five-hundred-rupee note. If your friends are like your family, life becomes wonderful. Varun, Malvika, Ahana and Garima were now part of one such crazy family that knew how to have fun without any limits.

Loves Me, Loves Me Not

'Why don't you convey your feelings to Malvika? I think she likes you too,' Ahana suggested, sipping her coffee.

It was late at night but Varun was still busy with his assignments in the living room. Two days had passed since their crazy road trip and they were again settling into their old routine. Keeping him company were Garima and Ahana who were watching television. Malvika was asleep in her bedroom. He blushed as soon as Ahana asked the question. He had been planning to confess his feelings to Malvika but was waiting for the right time.

'Tomorrow is a book launch in Mumbai.' He smiled.

'So?' Ahana asked.

'Oh shit. Are you serious?' Garima asked.

She understood what he meant. Malvika had told her about a book launch she was eager to attend but, in all probability, she was going to miss it due to her practical exams.

'What is happening?' Ahana seemed confused.

'Malvika loves reading and tomorrow is her favourite author's book launch in Mumbai. So I am going to attend it just so I can get an autographed copy of the book with a personal message for her from the author that will read, "Malvika, will you be Varun's girlfriend?"'

'That's a brilliant idea. She was really sad about missing the event. This will make her really happy,' Garima said in excitement.

Ahana loved the idea but what really delighted her was that he wanted to surprise Malvika with another out-and-out romantic gesture. He had dismissed it because he was short of cash but Ahana convinced him to borrow money from her and go ahead with his plans. After all, when you love someone you should not hesitate to express it wholeheartedly. He immediately called the concerned person to confirm the plan. He was scared that his plan would backfire but with Ahana and Garima's support, he was willing to take the chance. No wonder they were BFFs. Best friends make your problems and fears their own, so you don't have to face them alone.

You don't need to do any cardio exercises once your heart starts beating for someone. The best cardio is the way love makes your heart race. The most wonderful love stories are those in which you fall in love with the most unexpected person at the most unexpected time. Before coming to Mumbai, Varun had never expected to fall in love with his roommate.

Varun left for the book launch without informing Malvika about it. She had no idea what was coming her way. As he reached the bookstore, he saw a huge crowd waiting for the author to arrive. For a moment, he was disheartened thinking his plan wouldn't become reality, seeing the excitement of the fans who were waiting to click pictures and take autographs. Without thinking too much of the consequences, he purchased the book and waited for the author to arrive. The moment the author entered, girls started hooting and cheering for one glimpse of him. This depressed Varun even more. *Was Malvika in love with the author?* He waited patiently until the event was over and the anchor announced, 'The stage is open now. Those who want to take autographs can come ahead. But please maintain a single queue to avoid chaos.'

The author took the mike from the anchor and said, 'Guys, don't worry. Just come one by one in a queue. I will sign every single book and click photos too.'

As Varun heard this, he started jumping in joy. The girls standing next to him thought that he was another crazy fan. Their giggles hardly mattered to Varun. He stood in the queue patiently and waited for his turn.

'What's your name?' the author asked as soon as Varun handed over the book to him.

'I want you to write my friend's name. Malvika. Also, if you can add a message?' Varun requested.

Before the author could start writing a message of his own, Varun said, 'I want you to write "Will you be Varun's girlfriend, Malvika?"'

The author looked up and smiled at Varun.

'I hope she accepts your proposal. If so, do inform me. Hopefully I'll get an interesting story to write.'

'Sure,' Varun added and left. *Who the hell is going to reveal their story to this author?* he thought.

Without wasting any more time, he left the place.

Once he returned to Navi Mumbai, he went to the shop where he had ordered some T-shirts. The shop was about to close, but Varun managed to reach just in time. He called Ahana and asked if everything was ready. Ahana replied in the affirmative. He took out his wallet and glanced at the picture of his mother. Thankfully the picture was not in the wallet that was stolen on the road trip.

How desperately he wanted her to be with him but death is beyond anyone's control. He wiped the tears off his face and hailed a cab home. The book and the T-shirts were carefully hidden in his bag. After having dinner, Garima requested Malvika to join her for a walk.

'Are you okay?' Malvika asked.

'Of course.'

'Then all of a sudden why do you want to go for a walk?'

Everyone pretended like they didn't know anything.

'Something is cooking. Tell me!'

'Nothing. I just wanted some fresh air so I thought of going a walk. This pain is making me mad,' Garima said, faking a headache to convince Malvika.

Malvika finally agreed. As per the plan, Garima was to return not before an hour. As soon as they left, Varun took out the candles he had bought. Ahana was impressed by Varun's preparation. Both of them made the necessary arrangements in the living room.

'All the notes are ready, right?' Varun asked.

Ahana nodded and handed them to him. In the meanwhile, she lit the candles all around. The stage was set and all Varun had to do now was to speak his heart. He was very nervous about it and the nervousness showed on his face. You know, there are times when you want to ask that simple little question and then you realize you're afraid of that one simple little answer. Varun too was afraid of that one simple little answer.

'Dude, the way you have set up everything, if you propose to me right now, I will accept it.' Ahana laughed just to make him relax.

'Shut up. Let me message Garima that we are ready.'

He sent Garima a WhatsApp message. *Hey, you can come back. Everything is set. Just pray everything goes well. And yes, your T-shirt is in your bedroom. We both have ours on already.*

Once the message was delivered, he immediately logged on to Facebook and uploaded a status tagging Malvika. *It's going to be a memorable night for you. Because of you I smile a lot more these days. I think I have found my forever.*

He thought at least ten times before clicking 'Post'.

'Fuck! Fuck! Fuck!' was all he could scream once he posted the status. He refreshed his page almost a hundred times in just a minute just to check if Malvika had commented on it or even liked it. Sometimes we don't care how many people like our status. The only thing we care about is that the status reaches the one person it is meant for!

Love makes you do silly things. It can make you buy a book even if you are not interested in reading it. Because the happiness of your girl lies in reading that book. It makes you buy candles even when there is no power cut. Some people aren't just special, they are simply irreplaceable and Malvika was certainly one of those people for Varun.

Whenever he was with her, he wished the clock would turn anticlockwise or just stop moving altogether!

Malvika saw the Facebook notification just before she entered the apartment. She had a smile on her face after reading Varun's status. However, she was unaware of all that he had planned for her. As the door opened, she saw that the lights were dim and there were candles lit beautifully all over. Varun was standing there waiting to see Malvika's reaction, while she was absolutely speechless. Ahana was in the bedroom and as soon as Garima entered she went inside to change her T-shirt. Varun and Malvika were left alone in the living room. The air was filled with romance. Malvika saw a red velvet ribbon tied from one end of the room to the other. From it hung eleven little notes.

'Why don't you read them? They are all for you,' Varun said, breaking the silence.

Malvika couldn't believe all of this was actually happening to her. She went closer to the first note attached to the ribbon. It read: *You are the only perfect part of my imperfect life.*

Reading the first message, she blushed and looked back lovingly at Varun. Then she moved on, reading one note after another.

I will love you until oranges grow on apple trees!

Even in my darkest hours just the thought of you can brighten up my entire world!

You are the secret ingredient to my happiness.

The reason we found each other so late in life was to let us experience what we didn't want on our way to what we truly want.

You have given me a million reasons to love you since the day we met and every day you give me more!

Since I met you, I have earned a new degree—a 'Masters in Missing You'. The course has taught me all the different ways and different times to miss you.

I love it when I catch you looking at me, then you smile and look away.

Of all the people in the world . . . it's only you I can't stop thinking about!

I didn't find you, you didn't find me—we found each other!

Somewhere between crying for a doll and crying for a person you grew up to be a woman. But I will never let you cry for a person and I will make sure you carry your elegant smile always!

Her eyes welled up with tears. She looked up at Varun who smiled innocently, looking at her. Malvika ran to him and hugged him tightly. She tightened the grip as much as she could just to show him that this was not going to end soon. It was going to last until her last breath. One universe, eight planets, seven continents, over three hundred countries, over six billion people, and still they were lucky enough to meet each other! Varun released the grip, looked in her eyes and said, 'I feel so comfortable with you. Like I can share everything without thinking or manipulating. It's my first time and I know it's not yours. But that doesn't matter to me. I believe we can get along together and though we will fight, every morning it will feel so good to wake up knowing you are mine and I am yours. All I have is this fragile heart of mine and even though it has a few bruises, it still uses all its strength to love you and only you. Maybe I am acting a bit romantic, but I have never felt like this before. I am sorry if I am being a little cheesy, but once in a while it's fine, I suppose. You know you're in love when you just look at their Facebook pictures, and smile spontaneously, and just can't stop. That's what you do to me. You know how to make me smile and if you give me a chance, I want to make you feel the same way for the rest of your life. You have made me a better person and I want to be a part of your life for a lifetime.'

Malvika was blushing continuously. The best feeling in the world is knowing that you have a special place in the heart of someone special. Everything else just doesn't matter! Varun presented her with the book by her favourite author that he had had autographed especially for her. Malvika saw the personalized message and said, 'I never thought I would be so lucky.'

'To have the signed book or to have me in your life?' Varun smiled and told her to turn around. There they were—Ahana and Garima standing with their T-shirts on. Varun switched off all the lights in the room and came and stood next to Garima. The text on their T-shirts glowed.

Ahana had 'Will you' written on her T-shirt, Garima had 'be my' and Varun had 'girlfriend?' on his.

'So will you be my girlfriend?' Varun asked.

Malvika just nodded and gave him a tight hug. When you find a special someone who means everything to you, you hold on to them and cherish every moment you have with them!

'Let's move then. We hardly have ten minutes left,' Varun said, looking at his watch.

'What for?' Malvika asked in surprise.

'Wait and watch,' Garima said.

They locked the door and moved towards the terrace. Malvika was confused about what was happening but at the same time she was excited. Once they reached the terrace, everyone kept distracting her one way or the other so that she wouldn't look towards the sky.

'What exactly is it about Malvika that's so desirable?' Ahana asked Varun to keep Malvika engaged in conversation.

'It's everything about her. She is irresistible,' Varun replied.

'That's it?' Malvika asked.

'Everything about you is special. I can tell you one thing for sure. In future, no matter how different our opinions might be, I will still stand by you and love you, more than any man has ever loved you.'

The next second Varun held Malvika's hand and stood behind her, lifting her chin up so she would look towards the sky. The surprise was waiting for her! Varun had hired a skywriter! A skilled pilot in a plane was flying through the sky, the white smoke from his aircraft forming letters.

As she looked up, she could see the words 'I love you, Malvika' in the sky.

Once the words were formed the plane emitted more smoke in the shape of a heart around the words. Everyone started cheering and screaming Varun's and Malvika's names. Varun was content that everything had gone as the plan. For a moment he looked towards Ahana to thank her and she looked back and smiled. Malvika couldn't stop her tears as not even for a second had she thought something so grand was coming her way. The moment was priceless for her—larger than life. Sometimes, a lifetime spent with someone may be meaningless. But a moment spent with someone who really loves you is more than life itself.

Varun went closer to her and held her firmly by her waist.

'Until I met you, I thought the concept of having a person who lights up your entire life and makes every day seem brighter was just something that existed in movies. But now I know that you're the one I've been looking for all my life. When we first met I was afraid of letting you in, and I'm sure that you felt that too. I guess that deep down I was worried that I couldn't be everything you needed and were looking for. But little by little I see how you accept my flaws, and how patient you are with me. Whenever I talk to you, I feel like the luckiest guy in the whole wide world. There's nothing that I need to hide from you, nothing I can't tell you; there are no uncomfortable silences, no secrets and no judgements passed. While I'm opening myself up, I'll let you in on a little secret—you're the reason I strive to be a better person. I love you, Malvika.'

After his monologue, they kissed! The kiss seemed to last an eternity. Malvika slowly opened her eyes and parted her lips.

'There was something about you that attracted me from the very first day. Even though you were not really the social type, you told me everything about you—your home, family, your feelings. When you cried out your grief and sorrow to me, I felt so close to you. I wanted to engulf you in my arms and make you feel safe and secure. I felt extremely happy and proud to give you this support and comfort. And somewhere along the way, I opened my heart to you without even realizing so. Anything that made me happy or sad, I couldn't wait to share it with you. We both don't know how or when we slowly developed these feelings for each other. But know that it gives me great pride to show the world how madly I am in love with you.'

The best feeling in the world is not loving someone but to be loved by that same person. We all have that one person with whom we argue and fight, but we still cannot resist talking to them. Malvika and Varun were one such couple!

Men Will Be Men

The feeling of being in a relationship is the best feeling in the world. Varun and Malvika woke up with a similar feeling the next day. She had dozed off in his arms the previous night and would not let go of his hand even when he put her to bed. He had no option but to sleep next to her. While Malvika was still fast asleep, Varun lay next to her, looking at her with love. He gave her a quick peck on her cheeks and she opened her eyes. Varun and Malvika had decided to spend the whole day together because this was like their first date. A groggy-eyed Malvika got up and took Varun's hands in hers. Not because she was feeling romantic early in the morning, but because she wanted to convince Varun of one simple little thing most guys are scared of.

'Varun, since we have decided to spend some time together, I have a brilliant idea,' said Malvika in a seductive tone, her lips very close to his.

'And what's that?' Varun said, touching his lips to hers.

As they faced each other, Malvika kissed him passionately. The kiss was the first step in convincing him of her plan.

'It's something I've always wanted to do. I never got an opportunity in the past to—'

Varun interrupted Malvika and asked, 'Tell me what it is?'

'Let's go shopping!'

SHOPPING. The word most boyfriends fear to hear.

'Baby, why don't we go watch a movie instead? You can go shopping some other day. I mean we . . . we can go shopping some other day.'

'No, I want to go with you. Please, baby.'

Varun was trying his best to distract her. Suddenly, words like 'baby', 'sweetheart', 'princess', 'shona' were introduced in the conversation with the hope that the shopping plan would be dropped. Varun made a face of disgust similar to what one makes when faced with a difficult question in an exam.

I have enough clothes and shoes . . . said no girl ever! *They shop day in and day out and still have nothing to wear.*

If it were in their hands, they would build their bedrooms inside shopping malls, Varun thought.

Shopping is the cause of half the break-ups in the world. It's not shopping that irritates guys. What irritates them is that generally girls go to buy a suit but see a beautiful handbag and hence end up buying a sexy pair of shoes. Guys go shopping to buy what they want; girls go shopping to find out what they want. Varun tried his level best to distract her but failed and finally gave in just to make her happy.

Varun borrowed Ahana's car and they decided to go to Inorbit Mall, Vashi.

'Now I am convinced that I have made the right choice when it comes to boyfriends. I can go shopping with you all the time,' Malvika said, tightening her grip on his hand as they made their way into the mall.

'Of course. We can go shopping on every date. It would be so much fun,' Varun said, sarcastically.

Malvika gave him an angry look and started walking in the direction of Shopper's Stop. The afternoon of shopping terror had actually begun for Varun. At first, it seemed okay to him but after looking around for some outfits, Malvika started asking for advice. Varun was now super afraid to say anything wrong. Malvika picked up a top and asked him how it looked on her.

'Wow. Fantastic. Take it,' Varun said.

Everything she tried looked fantastic according to Varun even if it didn't. He was trying to speed up the buying process or they would be at the mall forever but his plan backfired because of her inability to choose from the countless outfits she had picked up.

'I will try out each one of them. You just sit here outside the changing room,' Malvika stated.

Varun's jaw dropped as there were nearly ten outfits in her hands. He just sat there and every time she came out he tried to put on a happy face. But after she had tried around five of them, Varun started to get annoyed and she could sense it.

'Baby, just a few more minutes. You want me to look hot in front of your friends, right? So tolerate this bit.'

Girls have done a PhD in the art of shopping, Varun thought.

He felt he had turned twenty years older since he had entered the mall.

'I wish every time I like an outfit on Instagram, it would magically appear in my closet,' Malvika said, coming out of the dressing room.

Just when he thought the ordeal was over, she decided to try one more outfit. Varun pushed her back inside the trial room and locked the door. He went closer to her and planted a kiss on her lips. The clothes she was holding in her hands fell to the ground.

'Baby, we're in a dressing—' she started to protest but it was too late.

He took off her top and bit her on the neck. She moaned in ecstasy. Just when she was about to unzip his pants, they heard another girl talking on the phone outside. They made sure they were extra quiet and Varun started saying things like, 'I like this one on you, but do you think a smaller size will fit you better? Should I go get one?'

Malvika couldn't control her laughter. She hurriedly put her top back on and came out of the dressing room. The girl was still talking on the phone and looked in Malvika's direction as she came out. Within a few seconds, she saw Varun coming out from the same dressing room and gave him a strange look. Varun smiled awkwardly at her and quickly went in the opposite direction. He helped Malvika choose a scarf and bag and they walked to the billing counter to pay for the items. Unfortunately, the same girl who had seen them come out of the dressing room was standing in front of them at the counter. She looked at them with utter disgust on her face. As Malvika left the store, she showed the girl the middle finger.

Finally, Malvika's shopping spree was over and the best part was that Varun had survived it. He had also bought himself a cool jacket in the process. As they left, Varun told her he had actually enjoyed the day even though he wasn't so sure in the beginning, and that he would love to go shopping every day if it was the same as today. Malvika blushed and both of them headed towards the parking lot.

The sun was about to set as Malvika guided Varun to Kharghar hills. It is a scenic location situated at the western side of the Kharghar township from where you get a helicopter view of the entire township. When they reached the top, Varun was amazed at the beauty of the place. He never knew that in such a crowded city as theirs, there existed a place so beautiful, away from the hustle and bustle of their lives. Varun and Malvika went for a walk together, hand in hand.

'Do you think your dad will accept our relationship?' Malvika asked as they rested on one of the rocks.

'I am not going to give him an option. It's my life and he has to accept our love. I have no fear of telling him about our relationship. After all, I love you and you are mine forever,' Varun said, coming close to her.

They hugged each other. His words of assurance made all the doubts in Malvika's mind vanish.

'I will keep telling you I love you until my last breath,' said Varun. Malvika was ready to sacrifice everything for Varun. She was madly in love and each second with him made her feel like she was a blessed soul. It's not hard to sacrifice something for someone but it's hard to find that someone who deserves your sacrifice. Varun deserved it all.

Minutes later, Varun took out his cell phone and logged on to his Facebook account. Malvika took a peek at his mobile phone and complained, 'Do you want to spend time with me or be on Facebook?'

'You have to love me the way I am.'

'You can at least leave Facebook alone while you are with me. Are you so addicted to it?'

'As if you are not! Every time you post a status or upload a photo, don't you tell me to comment on it?'

'We've hardly been in a relationship for a day and look at us fighting,' Malvika said in a sad tone. Varun just smiled and brought his mobile screen closer to her face. He had changed his relationship status from 'Single' to 'Committed'. This brought a smile on Malvika's face. These days if a guy uploads his relationship status on Facebook or shares his password with his girlfriend, it's considered a sign of loyalty. Varun had done exactly the same as he knew it would please Malvika and he had no shame in accepting that he was in a relationship.

'I wish there was an option of changing your relationship status to 'Trying to get into a fight with my girl, so that we can have passionate make-up sex later', teased Varun as he moved closer to her.

'Shut up,' Malvika chided, pushing him away.

Varun and Malvika ate at a nearby dhaba and left soon after as it was getting dark. On the way back home, Malvika rested her head on his shoulders. Never before had she felt so comfortable in her life. She had been in a relationship before and had confessed all about it to Varun. It didn't change Varun's outlook towards Malvika. Fate may decide your destiny. But the choices you make decide your fate. Malvika had made the right choice. Every girl deserves a man who makes her forget that her heart has been broken ever!

Once they reached their flat, Varun told her to go inside, saying he would meet her upstairs in a few minutes.

Malvika went upstairs while Varun went to a nearby pharmacy and bought a packet of condoms. He had a feeling tonight was going to be the night. Gathering all his courage, he walked back towards the apartment. It was their first time and he wanted to make it special. As he reached upstairs, he opened the door with his keys. He did not want to ring the bell and wake up Ahana and Garima. But luck didn't favour him as they were awake anyway. Malvika had woken them up to show them her new outfits. Varun stood there, sad and depressed. All his fantasies had come crashing down in no time. He sat quietly on the corner of the bed near the window as the girls checked out her new clothes.

'Even though I have Moods in my pocket, my girlfriend is in no mood to make out,' Varun thought dejectedly. He took the condom packet from the pocket of his jeans and quickly threw it outside the window.

'Why are you quiet? You can join us,' Ahana said to Varun.

'I've already had enough of this.' Varun reacted strongly, looking at Malvika.

He took out his mobile phone and sent her a message on WhatsApp, *We had planned something tonight. Forgot?*

Malvika glanced at Varun and gave him a naughty look. She replied, *Yes. I remember. I have something in mind. Let them sleep first.*

Varun messaged her back asking what she had in mind. She replied asking him to be patient. But Varun couldn't control his anxiety and messaged asking, *Is the plan on for tonight on or not?*

Malvika started giggling after which Ahana asked her what had happened. She made up a lie saying a friend had sent her a joke. Luckily, Ahana didn't ask her to read the message else Varun would have jumped from the window. Malvika nodded and Varun's excitement knew no bounds.

'I'll be back,' Varun said and ran out of the house.

Before anyone could ask where he was going, he had already shut the door. He ran down as fast as he could and reached the back of the apartment. He had come looking for the packet of condoms he had thrown away a few minutes ago. He continued his search for the next few minutes, but to no avail. He switched on the flashlight on his mobile and started looking again. Finally he was able to locate it! When he entered the apartment, he saw Ahana and Garima had gone into their respective rooms.

'How did you manage to do that?' Varun asked.

'I am smart—you have to agree.' She winked.

Varun immediately pulled her close and locked his lips with hers. Malvika pushed him away and told him to be patient. She took him to the terrace. Earlier, it was Varun who had given Malvika a surprise on the terrace, but now he was going to get one. He had no clue why they were going up.

Once they reached the terrace, he saw a bed sheet in a corner of the terrace, with candles lit all around it. Malvika locked the terrace door so that no one could come up and took Varun to the corner. Varun observed that the candles were arranged in the shape of the letters M and V, the initials of their names. He wondered how she had arranged things in such a short time. He had to accept that she was indeed smarter than he gave her credit for. She had planned to get cosy on an open terrace under the moonlight in the warmth of the candles.

He went towards her and planted moist kisses all over her body. The cold breeze made them even hornier.

His hands were seeking pleasurable places to stroke and caress her. One hand slipped effortlessly into her panties to make love to her womanhood, and as she became wet and opened in invitation, he explored the velvety dew of her pink enclave. She had nothing to do but to lie back, close her eyes and submerge herself in a pool of pleasure.

'You are so wet . . . and it's turning me on. Don't scream. Somebody may hear us.'

'It's already three in the morning. No one will hear even my loudest moans,' she teased as he fingered her. He pushed Malvika down to the ground and unzipping his jeans, said, 'I don't have to teach you what to do.'

Wanting to reciprocate, to share the sensuous delight in which she was thoroughly immersed, she reached for him to explore his full length, running her fingers up and down, loving the way he responded to her touch, listening to his moans of approval, the way he verbalized his passion, fondling him, rubbing him until he was slippery to the touch. She parted her legs and he inserted his manhood into her depths, taking them both over the most heavenly edge. When it was over, she thought they would just cuddle and sleep, but he kept touching and caressing her, as if reluctant to let the flames of passion diffuse.

'You are an amazing lover,' she said a few hours after their passionate lovemaking session. 'You know sex boosts your immune system better than orange juice.'

'Then let's have sex every day. We won't have to take medicines ever. I want to make love to you in every room of our house. Would you like that?'

She wanted to say 'Oh yes' but the pragmatic side of her responded first, 'You know Ahana and Garima stay in the same house. We can't do that.'

'I know,' he said, disappointed, 'but it's worth dreaming about.'

As they lay on the ground facing the sky, she silently took Varun's hand and placed it on her stomach.

'You know some day I will have a life in there,' she said and a tear fell from her eye. 'And imagine how happy my husband would be when I tell him that his baby is inside my womb and the next nine months will be tough for him. Medicines, early-morning walks, pregnancy clubs and whatnot. And then, after a long struggle, he or she will finally come out and . . . and . . . and . . .'

Malvika almost ran out of words and Varun took the lead. 'And he will call me "Dad".'

'Will you just be the kid's father or my husband too?'

'You don't need to ask such a question. I breathe for you and my life is all yours. No one can take your place ever. It's the small things that matter in life. Like waking up and realizing that you finally got laid last night.'

'You're such a dog,' Malvika complained, much to Varun's amusement.

Varun and Malvika had experienced their first time together. A real relationship has fights. Has trust. Has faith. Has tears. Has hurt. Has smiles. Has genuine laughter. Has imperfections and has unconditional love! Varun and Malvika had met by chance and now they couldn't imagine their lives without each other. True love is not finding the perfect person, it's finding that someone who is just as messed up as you are and making a messed-up future together!

Unexpected Moments

Examination fever was all around, with the exams beginning in a fortnight. Varun was fast asleep in his room, tired after the previous night's long make-out session. Ahana was frustrated as all the rooms were messy. She decided to clear the clutter so she wouldn't misplace her important notes. She burst into Varun's room and kicked him fiercely when she found his socks under the kitchen table. Consequently Varun got up with a hurting rear.

'Can't you keep your socks in the correct place? Every time I find them scattered around, never in the place where they belong. On the kitchen table, in the sink, stuffed in pockets!'

It has long been established that losing socks is one of the bizarre evolutionary quirks that guys have developed over the years. Varun was no different. He looked around for Malvika but she had gone to the grocery store. Not paying much heed to Ahana's complaining, he headed for the washroom.

'I will be cooking today. You girls can take the day off and leave it to me. I will churn out some finger-licking stuff,' Varun announced.

Ahana and Garima stared at him for a moment, then burst out in chorus, 'Is this the after-effect of love?'

'Not really,' Varun replied from inside the washroom.

'Did you ever lust for Malvika? Tell me the truth.'

'Oh please! No harm in loving and lusting for the same person,' Varun replied, still in the washroom.

'What's the difference?' Garima asked.

'Love is when Malvika wears the dress Varun gifted her.' Ahana winked.

'And lust?'

'When she wears nothing underneath it.' Ahana laughed.

Varun came out in a flash and threw a towel at Ahana to shut her nonsense. Malvika was yet to return and Ahana was in a cheerful mood, nagging Varun.

'You are lucky not to have had any previous relationships. Else it would be difficult to find a girl with the same name,' she added.

'Why would I be dating a girl with the same name as my ex?'

'See, if you date someone with the same name as your ex, there's no chance of calling out the wrong name when you are making out,' Ahana responded.

Garima laughed, looking at Varun who was now chasing Ahana. Just then the bell rang and Malvika came in.

'Varun is the cook for the day!' Ahana announced.

'Really?'

'Yes. But I'll cook only for you. No food for them!' a frustrated Varun exclaimed.

Garima laughed and added, 'Anyhow, we are looking forward to a delicious meal!'

'Varun cooks really well. He had cooked once when both of you were in college. It was simply wow,' Malvika said, kissing Varun on his cheek.

The teasing continued for a while before Ahana suggested that they have a party celebrating Varun and Malvika's relationship. Varun, Malvika and Garima were reluctant about it—there was hardly any time left for the exams and no one had studied seriously. They had just completed their internals on time but had not even gone through the syllabus. Varun still had journals to complete and assignments to submit. Though Ahana too had submissions coming up, she managed to convince everyone to party.

'Four neat drinks are not a joke,' Varun said while going through the menu.

The party had begun at Angrezi Pub in CBD, Belapur—an opulent pub with the perfect ambience for a party.

'Don't just look at the menu! Order something. In fact order anything at random, I can have it all,' Ahana stated.

Varun smiled and ordered the drinks. Happy hours were on and they were getting one drink free with every order.

'Now that's what makes every Indian happy. Buy one get one free, flat 50 per cent off, Tatkal ticket confirmation, winning a cricket match and happy hours at lounges,' Malvika exclaimed.

'Indeed, darling,' said Ahana as she high-fived Malvika.

They insisted that Garima join them for drinks. Garima resisted. She had never consumed alcohol with them before, but since Varun and Malvika kept insisting, she gave in.

'This time is never going to come back. So drink, fall in love, crush on a new guy every day. Express your feelings. Dream big. Let your imagination loose. Be impulsive. Go crazy. Flirt around. Get your heart broken. Dance madly even if you don't know how. Click photos in crazy poses. Laugh out loud. Just say what you want. Sing your favourite songs, shout, wander late at night, break the rules, drink as much as you can with your BFF, come up with your own philosophies, smile and make others smile, go for it. Live this age. Live this moment. Cheers, guys!' Varun declared.

'Because things are only going to get worse. Life will be difficult and your friends will be too busy to indulge in this mindless fun,' Garima added as she sipped her drink.

'Garima, what do you expect from your partner?' Malvika asked.

'A good salary.'

'Darling, the person should be honest. A salary is like your period. It comes once in a month and lasts for about five or six days! And then again the same cycle repeats itself.'

'Agreed, but if your period doesn't come, it means that you are in big trouble.' Garima laughed.

They were having a ball of a time, enjoying their drinks and celebrating life. Garima had gulped down five shots in quick succession. At first she felt tipsy, then she excused herself to go to the washroom.

When Varun offered to accompany her to the door, she refused saying that she could manage just fine.

As she reached the washroom and opened the door, someone patted her on the back. The door was half open and the washroom was vacant.

'Hey, what are you doing here?' she asked with a slight smile in her drunken state.

He didn't utter a word, just looked around to make sure no one was watching them. Then he pushed her in and bolted the door. Due to the effects of alcohol, everything seemed blurry to her. She couldn't understand what was happening.

The guy didn't want to rape her. But he wanted to teach her how the game was played. He didn't want to molest her but he wanted her to know what it was like to lose one's dignity. He wanted to make her realize the pain of losing yourself in the process of losing someone.

If you don't put your ugly past behind you, the memories rot, turning into obsession and revenge, and he was doing just that. Garima was the reason he was humiliated, his pride destroyed. He knew that what he did wasn't right but the issue could have been dealt with better, nobody had to get hurt. He wasn't hurt because of a broken relationship; he was hurt because the girl had walked out on him. His ego was bruised, and that bruised ego got the better of him and the world around him.

It's always the same story—if a guy initiates the break-up, he is termed a cool dude but if the girl does so, she is termed a bitch, whore and whatnot. It doesn't matter who is at fault or what the reason is behind the separation. Even if the guy is at fault and the girl breaks up with him, the guy will spare no chance to demean her and talk ill about her.

Sid was no different. He sought Ahana's attention and when he couldn't get past her emotional strength and saw her happy with her friends, he was more bitter than ever. His ego crushed, he remembered how Ahana had exclaimed, 'If you treat me like a game, I'll show you how it's played.' His friends poked fun at him and he felt humiliated, hence the revenge. He clicked a few offensive pictures of Garima, saying, 'Now I will teach you how to play this game. I could have raped you and hurt you physically but I want to torture you mentally and ruin your life every day.' Sid laughed.

Though he had no intention of harming her physically, he knew what he had done would crush her mentally and emotionally. This was his way of taking revenge on Ahana. He peeked outside and saw that everyone was busy mingling. He came out of the washroom cautiously and left the pub.

An abused person can never fully recover from a traumatic experience. Garima slowly managed to walk back to their table.

'What took you so long?' Varun asked.

'Sid . . .'

The name shocked everyone. Ahana was dumbstruck.

'Did he say something to you? Did he touch you?' Varun asked in a furious tone.

'No. But . . . he was . . . talking . . . about some game . . . about mentally torturing us . . .' Garima stammered. Ahana and Varun didn't have a good feeling about it. They cleared the bill and left at once. Malvika asked Garima several questions on their way back home but couldn't get a proper response. Varun's intuition said that something had gone horribly wrong. Ahana too was scared. They didn't have a clue as to what Sid was up to. None of them were able to get much sleep that night.

The hardest thing to accept is the realization that the one you love has stopped loving you. Sid couldn't accept it and had decided to take revenge in the most horrible way.

'Malvika, wake up. Fast. For God's sake,' Varun shouted.

'Why are shouting early in the morning? What's wrong?' Malvika questioned.

Ahana, still yawning, looked at Varun anxiously. She had crashed in their room last night. Varun handed over the phone to Malvika to show her the horror he had woken up to. Malvika couldn't believe her eyes. She passed the phone to Ahana with trembling hands and Ahana went numb looking at it. Varun had received a video on WhatsApp in which Sid was kissing Garima. It was a short clip, barely five seconds long. Ahana and Malvika checked their phones and saw that they too had received the same clip from Sid. They were sure that Sid had sent the clip to Garima as well. Varun thought of deleting the video from her phone before Garima could see it.

However, her door was locked from the inside. They had sensed something fishy at the lounge but had not expected something as nasty as this.

Within minutes, everyone received a message from Sid: *'I could have done something worse like circulating this on the Internet, but not yet. Wait for the right time. Get ready to play the game. Play for your life.'*

'How could he? I am not going to let that moron get away with this. Son of a bitch!' Ahana shouted.

'This is not the right time. Calm down,' Varun stated.

'We shouldn't have made her drink. It's entirely our fault. What are we supposed to do now? It's over if it goes viral,' Malvika cried.

Everyone looked at each other. There was silence all around. Somewhere they were aware that this was the beginning of a nightmare for them. A nightmare from which they could not wake up. Life's dark side had caught up with them.

Varun considered entering Garima's room and deleting the clip from her phone, but he was a bit hesitant.

They were all overwhelmed by what was happening, unable to process their emotions. Receiving this video had suddenly applied the brakes on all the fun they'd been having, completely distorting their happy memories.

As Varun moved about the living room anxiously, he glanced at his diary and opened it to see what he had written some time ago when he was missing his mom.

She gave life. She will be someone's wife.
She is a girlfriend and someone's best friend.
She is a sister and a survivor to the end.
She works, cooks and cleans.
She laughs, helps, comforts, and hides her pain.
When you struggle she pulls you through and helps you again.

All of this is she and what do we do?
Complain and create a mess.
Provide stress and leave her feeling depressed.
Push her away and ignore her advice.
Tell her she is nothing without thinking twice.

She was tortured and abused.
You clicked offensive videos and photographs of her,
Told her she was nothing and would always be used.
Making her cry was a game to you.
One should respect women, but how could you?

She swallows her pride, puts her feelings aside.

Ignores your ignorance and tolerates your flaws and takes your side.

You call her bitch, slut, ho and tramp,
She answers with pride and dignity like a champ.
You call her nothing.

But I call her strong, smart, sensual, caring, giving, a survivor, tolerant and powerful.

I call her a Woman!

One thing was proven that day, that women were made to feel weak by men who hurt their dignity and pride, hitting them where it hurts the most. Who is to blame? The man who makes her feel hopeless and weak by treating her like an object just because his ego is bruised? The girl who allows the man to make her feel hopeless by treating her like an object? Or a society that has always portrayed girls as weak, their honour an easy target?

When Nothing Goes Right

'I think we should delete the message from her cell phone. She will get depressed if she sees it. I know her well,' Malvika said, fearing the worst.

'But the room is—'

Before Ahana could finish, Malvika interrupted saying she was extremely worried for Garima who had always kept her distance from strangers. She was convinced that it was not her fault and she had been trapped for no reason.

'I am not going to let that bastard go! But how do I show Garima this? He won't circulate the video; he doesn't have guts to do that. I have lived with him and I know how his mind works,' Ahana said, pacing up and down.

A hush descended over them as the three gradually moved towards Garima's room, which was still locked.

Ahana got the master key from her room so that they could sneak in and delete the message before Garima woke up and saw it. It would be a huge task to make her forget about the incident as there was something that had always haunted her, something she hadn't revealed to anyone. The painful memories of her past were still fresh in her mind and with this tragedy, it seemed like recovery would take even more time. Malvika knew her the best and felt she would go into depression as she was not mentally strong and this could result in a complete nervous breakdown. Everyone knew she was innocent and hence wanted to shield her from this, especially when she had exams coming up.

Varun took the key from Ahana and inserted it into the keyhole. Once the door was unlocked, he pushed it open as quietly as possible. As the door opened, they couldn't believe the scene in front of them.

Garima lay unconscious in a pool of blood with her left wrist slashed. The blood gushed from her wrist and she lay there face down, her wrist stretched over the pillow. She would have lost a few quarts by now. Everyone panicked and screamed, trying to wake Garima up, not knowing whether she was just unconscious or dead. Varun told Malvika and Ahana to bring some cold water to splash on her face. He took a handkerchief and wrapped it around her wrist to try and stop the bleeding but he couldn't.

Her wound was so deep and wide that at first it seemed impossible that the bleeding would stop.

What am I going to do now? I am certainly not going to watch her bleed to death, Varun thought.

When someone commits suicide, their entire family and friend circle plunges into confusion and grief. Life is instinctively valued by everyone. Even a blade of grass or flower fights for the privilege of life. When someone close to you voluntarily ends their life, your entire value system is thrown for a loop. Varun, Ahana and Malvika felt guilty, thinking they somehow should have seen the signs that led Garima to take this step. Hope—a word most people have to hold on to tightly because if it slips out of their fingertips, it is gone forever. Garima had lost hope, thinking she had committed a sin. They watched the blood—her blood—drip off her pale skin and soak into the bed sheet. They splashed some water and checked if she was still breathing. She was! She was still alive, but barely. She had sought to escape the cruelty in the world when she could no longer cope with it but she left her friends shattered by choosing that route.

Varun picked her up with Malvika's help. Ahana ran down to fetch the car from the parking space. They rushed towards the hospital. Ahana drove as fast as she could. All of them prayed to God to give Garima the strength to carry on. Their lives had just begun, so how could hers end? They would fight with the world for her but wouldn't let her die such a death. She didn't deserve it. As Malvika looked at Garima's pale face, she found a piece of paper sticking out of the pocket of her track pants. She took it out and read it.

I'm not sure why I'm writing this. I was raised in a family where I went to the temple every Sunday and was taught the importance of faith and God in our lives. It doesn't matter. It doesn't help me. I was hurt . . . badly . . . when I was a child. I was hurt in a way that no person, no little child, should be hurt. I thought about ending my life that time. I have been hospitalized for attempts before. I have been put on medication to help with the depression. I never told any of you about it. It's not worth telling. It's something I wanted to erase forever. But couldn't. Now this MMS! I don't know whether you will trust me or not but I didn't do anything. Ahana, will you believe me? Don't be mad at me please. You are my best friend. How could I? I feel certain that I am going mad again. I feel I can't go through another of those terrible times. I shall not recover this time. All of you helped me a lot to overcome my past. Just when I wanted to give up, you made me believe in life once again. Life is so confusing . . . what we want we don't get, what we get we are not satisfied with, what we expect never happens and what we hate happens again and again. I have the urge to justify my actions, but I assume I'll never be able to convince anyone that this was the right decision. Maybe it's true that anyone who does this is insane by definition. Maybe you won't stop wondering why I did this. Since I've never spoken to anyone about what happened to me, you may draw your own conclusions but the fact is, I can't face the world now. My past torture was personal; however with this MMS they will now call me a slut, a whore and whatnot. But my heart knows I am innocent and doesn't need to give an explanation.

I am sick of it all. Why should I bother trying any more? I'm not even afraid of dying. I'm not afraid of pain. I just want to leave this world. Please pray for me. I'm tired of trying. You see, I can't even write this note properly. Ahana, always stay the way you are—bold, fearless and strong. Malvika, always carry a smile—now that you have Varun to take care of you. And Varun, forgive your dad if possible. Yes, Malvika told me. Please don't misunderstand me, guys. The three of you are my family.

Malvika couldn't control her tears as she finished reading the letter. Their world had come to a standstill. She remembered what Garima had said once: *If you point the camera away from yourself just once, you just might find someone interesting on the other side.*

We are so lost in our own lives that sometimes we ignore what others might be going through. The hardest thing is knowing that your relationship is falling apart and realizing that you are losing what held you together.

As soon as they reached Sea Woods Hospital, Garima was taken to the emergency room. Malvika and Ahana waited outside while Varun completed all the necessary formalities. The few hours that it took the doctors to operate on her seemed like the longest hours of their lives. Life is so unpredictable. The previous night Garima was enjoying herself with all of them, clueless that the next day she would be on a hospital bed fighting for her life. Everyone felt miserable and heartbroken.

After some time, the doctors came out. All three of them stood up immediately, hoping for a miracle. When someone close to you is admitted in hospital, you feel helpless looking at their condition because there is nothing you can do to make things better. The thought of whether the person will come back home or will leave you forever haunts your mind. For the last few hours, they had tried every possible way to convince the Almighty that they needed Garima and it was neither the right time nor the right way to end things. Each step the doctor took towards them made their hearts beat faster. He stood in front of them and, with a smile, said, 'She is out of danger. Don't worry. But we need to keep her under observation for twenty-four hours at least. Please inform her parents.'

They breathed a sigh of relief and thanked the Almighty for making this possible. If they had not opened the door at the right time, things could have been worse. But Garima's time had not come yet. Her friends had put up a fight with God himself. Varun, Malvika and Ahana hugged each other with happiness and asked the doctor if they could see Garima. He permitted them to see her and everyone walked towards her room. Tears streamed down Varun's face; he had no words. They had been friends for a short while but they had all developed an unbreakable bond. In any case, they were not going to let Garima shut her eyes. No way were they ready to say goodbye!

It's never easy to see your friends and loved ones on a hospital bed, tubes sticking out of their arms. Malvika felt terrible as she was emotionally more attached to Garima. With a heavy heart, she saw her lying on the bed like a lifeless being. Tears rolled down her cheeks. Ahana went close and touched Garima's forehead. Garima slowly opened her eyes and saw everyone standing in front of her.

She was semi-conscious and felt extremely weak, since she had lost a lot of blood. She managed a smile and mumbled a feeble sorry for putting them in such an awkward place. She wanted to explain why she had taken such a drastic step but couldn't move or say much. Ahana told her not to waste her energy and to rest. Garima glanced at Malvika who was breaking out in sobs and as their eyes met, she too couldn't control her emotions. Malvika had never seen Garima so silent and helpless, it made her feel hopeless. It's said that two girls can't be true BFFs, but that was certainly not true in Malvika and Garima's case.

Malvika rushed out of the room in tears. Varun followed to console her as she stood crying in a corner.

'I know it's tough but she is absolutely fine now. If we don't keep our composure, how will we handle her? She needs us,' Varun said, hugging Malvika.

'I know, but I can't see her like this. Can't we take her home? I will tend to her. I will give her love enough to replace all the medicines. I will take care of her,' Malvika cried.

'Yes. We will take her home soon. Don't worry. But for that you have to be strong. If the doctor sees you in this condition, he'll never agree to send Garima home,' Varun said, trying to calm her down.

Varun gave her a glass of water and made her sit for a while. It was a difficult phase for everyone but they had to stand like rocks and let it pass. Ahana felt guilty and was upset because Sid was her ex-boyfriend and he was at the root of this turmoil. She kept blaming herself and wanted to beg Garima for forgiveness.

After Varun and Malvika had left the room, Garima signalled to Ahana to come close. They hadn't spoken a single word yet and Ahana couldn't even make eye contact. She went close and looked at Garima who whispered in her ear, 'I am sorry. I didn't do it. I wish I had died. If you think I did—'

Ahana placed a finger on her lips.

'Don't make me feel even more guilty. It's not your fault. Even if the Almighty swears that you did something I wouldn't believe it. Even if you had confessed, I would have taken it as a joke. I trust you more than myself. I know you well enough to know that you didn't do anything. It was all Sid's fault. In fact, I feel guilty. Because of me, you had to suffer. It should be me lying in this bed. You don't deserve this. I am really sorry. Forgive me,' Ahana cried.

The girls hugged each other. Ahana was strong but not impassive. She felt strongly for her friends, it was evident. A single moment of misunderstanding is toxic, because within a minute it can make us forget the hundred lovable moments spent together. However, they had no hard feelings or misunderstandings. Relationships are built with love, trust and caring.

Varun went back into the room with Malvika and stood beside Garima. She knew she had done something unforgivable.

'Friendship is a full-time responsibility. Not just when it is convenient for you. We never thought you would take such a hasty step without even discussing your troubles with us once. Life has given you a second chance. It doesn't always. Never do this again. Never. I may not have told you this but you are like my sister and I love you for who you are. I know you are stronger than this,' Varun said, holding Garima's hand.

'I won't leave you all so easily,' Garima said with a slight smile, trying to ease the tension.

'You bitch! Never do that. How will I live without you? You ass. I will fuck the shit out of you.' Malvika wept and hugged Garima. They loved each other unconditionally.

All four of them not only valued each other's company, they also looked out for each other in turbulent times. Today they were each other's strength. It's not about how many friends you have; it's all about how much those few friends love you and care about you.

Last Slice of Pizza

'Are you feeling better now?' Malvika asked Garima as she woke her up for dinner.

Malvika and Varun had successfully diverted her attention from the video clip. Ahana too was pampering her but was worried that Garima's condition might deteriorate as she wasn't eating properly. Malvika had tried informing Garima's parents but unfortunately they were not in town and their alternate numbers were not reachable. They were supposed to be back after a couple of weeks and hence she had left a message for them on voicemail. Garima, however, was upset about Malvika contacting her parents as she had always kept her distance from them.

Due to the heavy dose of medicines Garima felt drowsy and had slept for a few hours. Her hand hurt a bit but she felt comfortable otherwise.

'When are they discharging me?' she asked.

'Tomorrow afternoon,' Malvika replied, serving her the food provided by the hospital.

Garima felt the urge to eat something spicy. The hospital meals were too tasteless and bland. The rules did not allow outside food for patients and they had to consume only the food prescribed by the doctors at the hospital. But Garima hardly ate any of the hospital food. She revealed that she felt like eating pizza and pasta and garlic bread.

'Don't worry. I will do something,' said Varun and left.

Ahana sat beside Garima and asked her, 'Don't you want to meet your parents?'

'I guess not.'

'But why? You can tell them everything now.'

'I just feel they left me to suffer. You won't understand. Please let's j…j…just change the topic,' she stammered.

Ahana could feel her hands tremble at the very mention of her family. Emotions have a language of their own. Garima had kept all her past memories to herself, and even though these memories haunted her, she never could open up to anyone. She could never get rid of the horror. Malvika tried to distract her by clicking a few selfies.

'This one is so cool. I am uploading it,' Malvika said in excitement.

'You will never change.'

'I'm my favourite,' said Malvika, reciting Kareena's dialogue from *Jab We Met*.

All of them laughed and Ahana added, 'If these doctors allow two people to stay here tonight, I am sure Varun and you won't miss the opportunity to make out even here.'

'It will be thrilling. Especially in front of Garima while she is fast asleep.' Malvika winked.

Garima finally had a smile on her face. That's what they were aiming for with their senseless talk. Just then Varun entered with a backpack on his shoulders. Everyone looked at him in confusion.

'Are you planning to go to college?' Malvika seemed surprised.

'Of course not. But I am in a mood to party. And what can be more adventurous than a party in a hospital room?'

He opened his bag to reveal not college books but boxes of BBQ chicken pizza, pasta in red sauce and garlic bread with cheese. Garima looked at him wide-eyed and said that if a nurse or a ward boy walked in, they would land in serious trouble for breaking the rules. But Varun was not made to follow rules and he was ready to face the consequences if any. He just wanted to cheer everyone up, and there is nothing better than some delicious food to knock out the blues. Varun locked the door from the inside so that no one could enter, and opened the boxes, placing them on the table in front of Garima. Everyone pounced on it as if they hadn't eaten pizza for a decade.

'Now this is the life. And you wanted to end it,' Varun said, glancing at Garima.

Garima gave him an apologetic look. Her friends meant more to her than family and were trying their best to pamper her, doing the things she loved. They knew she was a foodie and were indulging her cravings.

The last piece of pizza remained and they were looking at each other, wondering who was going to grab it first. Generally they would have put up a fight over the last slice but today they insisted that Garima eat it. Within minutes all the food was over. Varun took a can of air freshener and sprayed it all over the room. He put all the empty boxes back into his bag and unlocked the door. A few minutes later the doctor came on his rounds. Everyone sat glued to their places as if nothing had happened.

'How are you feeling now?' the doctor asked, checking Garima's pulse rate.

'Now, I'm actually feeling better.' Garima winked at Varun.

The doctor smiled and, after discussing the reports with the nurse, was about to leave when he sensed something fishy. He caught the lingering aroma of pizza in the room. But unsure about it, he asked Varun if something was wrong.

'Yes doctor, I actually ordered one pizza, they sent two. I ate four slices and eight are still left.'

'What?' the doctor asked, surprised.

'You didn't hear me? See, I actually ordered one pizza, they sent two. I ate four slices and eight slices are still left.'

Ahana interrupted their conversation to avoid further complications, saying, 'Doctor, just ignore him. Actually he's gone crazy ever since Garima landed up here. You see, they are dating and he loves Garima so much that he can't see her in pain.'

Malvika shot a surprised look at Ahana who signalled to her to be quiet.

'But in the morning I saw this guy with *that* girl in the waiting lounge and they seemed pretty close,' the doctor remarked, pointing towards Malvika.

'That's right. Actually he is in love with both girls. He was dating Malvika but for the past few months he has also been seeing Garima. Phew! Let me clear this up. The three of them are actually figuring out who they are more compatible with,' said Ahana.

'Sorry, doctor,' said Varun. 'I won't drink henceforth. Actually I have a tendency to fart a lot after drinking. That must be my fart you smell.'

The doctor was close to being driven mad. He was about to leave when Varun stopped him again and whispered, 'Doctor, the best thing about being heavily drunk is that you save a lot of electricity. I haven't switched on the fan, and it's still rotating at this speed.'

The doctor gave him a disgusted look and left.

Varun smiled and closed the door. All of them burst out laughing. Garima actually felt better after all the reckless fun. When life gets too serious, you need someone with whom you can always be stupid! Ahana, Garima, Malvika and Varun acted stupidly, knowing they had to lower the intensity of the situation. Garima thanked the Almighty for sending such people in her life, people who could make her soul smile.

Garima was discharged the next day but was advised to rest for a week which worked to her advantage as she could study for the upcoming exams. Everyone took proper care of her and with each passing day she recovered. With their love and support, she had started to live again. But somewhere she was still worried about the clip that Sid had sent. She discussed the issue with Ahana who assured her that everything was under control.

'Don't worry, I've known that son of a bitch for a long time. He may have recorded you but he does not have the guts to circulate the video. If he had it in him, he would have done it by now. But he is a coward. He just knows how to harass people and he wants attention. I ignored him to such an extent that his ego took a fall and hence he played this cheap trick.'

'Are you sure?' Garima asked in fear.

'Yes. And obviously we are not going to let him get away with it. But our first priority is your health. So get well soon. We have to kick his ass together,' Ahana comforted Garima.

Varun too consoled her and gave her medicines while she played games on her cell phone to distract herself. He told her that everyone trusted her without a doubt. Varun and Ahana managed to calm her but not for long. She saw her mobile ringing and picked up the call. It was an unknown number but the voice on the other end was not unknown. She started shivering. She couldn't manage to speak a word.

'I will expose you. If you don't believe me then you can check your WhatsApp messages.'

The phone got disconnected. With a heavy heart, she managed to look at the mobile screen.

'1 WhatsApp message received.'

It read, *'You have just 2 choices. Do as I say or face the consequences.'*

A few pictures and a video accompanied the message. What had happened a few days ago was a mere trailer compared to what she saw in this message. Varun tried asking what was happening but Garima was devoid of any emotion. She looked dazed. He snatched the phone from her and what he saw shattered the ground beneath his feet.

There were a series of nude images of Garima! Varun realized that her face had been cropped from the video of Sid and her and Photoshopped on to the naked bodies.

He became furious and wanted to call the cops but Garima didn't want them involved because she feared they would question her character instead of helping her. She didn't want to revisit her past. She sobbed heavily on Ahana's shoulder, cursing her life.

She thought she had escaped the torture. Women are always thought of as the fragile sex, but nothing is as easily wounded as a man's ego. When Malvika came home, she sat with Ahana, Varun and Garima to discuss what had happened.

'Who made the phone call?' she asked.

'It's not important.'

'Why? What are you hiding? Why are you playing with your life?'

'I am not. It's not important who called but rather what he said.'

They were all shocked when Garima told them about her conversation with the caller. He was blackmailing Garima to sleep with her. He threatened to make the photos and the video go viral, not just among the students of her college but on the Internet as well, if she didn't agree. The other option he had presented her with was to pay him four lakh rupees in a couple of weeks. He knew Garima would not be able to arrange that huge an amount in such a short span of time and would be forced into giving in to his first demand. Under such circumstances it is natural to question the very existence of a supreme power. This was a test of not just her character, but also her moral fibre and her existence.

'I really think we should approach the cops and let them handle it,' Varun tried convincing them.

'No way. Being a girl I know what it takes to file a complaint. They will ignore the case and instead ask questions about why I am sharing an apartment with a guy, what I was doing late at night at a pub, etc. Our society is not yet that liberal. Be it cops or your neighbours, they all narrow-minded. Please understand my concerns. I beg you,' Garima cried.

'I think she is right. Your character is seen as inversely proportional to the amount of cleavage you show. Approaching cops induces fear instead of a sense of security. We shouldn't involve the cops. Also, look at her condition. She is shivering at the mere thought of it,' Malvika said, holding on to Garima.

'I will not accept his first choice. I would rather die than do that.'

'Of course, darling, it will be a matter of shame for us if we tell you to sleep with him. I really wish I could chop his dick off and serve it to him for dessert.'

'Let's just agree to his second demand. We will give him the money. He will destroy my life otherwise.'

'But is it Sid? I will screw his life, just tell me once. Sid is a coward. He won't do anything,' Ahana yelled.

The discussion continued for some more time. No one wanted Garima to agree to the first choice. Eventually she was successful in convincing everyone about not approaching the cops or anybody outside their group. The only option left was to agree to give the four lakh rupees he had asked for.

'But I don't have so much money with me right now. Moreover, if I ask my dad or if he finds out that I have made a transaction worth four lakhs on a single day, we will land in big trouble. We need to think of some other way to arrange the money.'

'Even Varun's savings won't be enough. Garima, how are we going to arrange for such a big amount? We are students and getting four lakh rupees is next to impossible,' Malvika said in a dejected tone.

Everyone turned towards Varun who was lost in thought. He looked at them and said that if they had no choice but to pay the money, there was only one way. Whether it was the right thing to do was for time to decide. But for now he had decided to stand by it. Varun's plan was to leak a university examination question paper!

'Have you gone nuts? Do you have the slightest idea how risky this is?' Ahana screamed.

Garima and Malvika didn't utter a word for some time. There was pin-drop silence in the room until Malvika broke the silence. 'How's that possible?'

'My seniors used to leak the university papers a day before the exam and sell them to a few students for a good amount of money. They used to do it so secretly that no one ever found out. I am sure we can sell them and collect enough money.'

'Is it safe?'

'I think so. They were never caught. We can surely take a chance now that we have no choice.'

'I am up for it,' Garima muttered.

It was a huge risk, their careers were at stake. But they were willing to go to any lengths for Garima.

Fulfilling the caller's demand was indeed a bad idea but they agreed to do it for Garima's sake.

Varun had managed to convince himself and the others of this plan even though he knew that if his father got the slightest hint of it, he would be dead. What do you do when all you want is to do something for yourself, but are so used to doing things for everyone else that you don't know what it is that you want.

It was final now—they were going to leak a university examination paper.

Breaking the Rules

One has to be strong when life throws difficulties at you. But no one tells you what the hell you have to do to be strong. It's not easy; emotions and feelings do not die natural deaths.

Varun knew that he had chosen the wrong path but every other road led to a dead end. What was he supposed to do? Supporting a friend in trouble was a good thing to do, but supporting them by wrong means—was that right? Was that acceptable? It's very easy to choose between right and wrong but your brain stops functioning when you have to choose between two wrongs. He could either leave Garima to her fate or rescue her from the mess by acquiring the money, by hook or by crook. He chose the latter.

'Are you certain the plan will work? We don't want any more complications.' Malvika was visibly tense.

'Yes. Still, just to be sure, I am going to meet the senior who accomplished this task before. I'm not going to reveal anything to him, just get the lab assistant's name, the one who helped them,' Varun said confidently.

'But who will buy the question paper from us?' Garima asked.

'I have already sent a WhatsApp message to a few close friends of mine who have shared it with their contacts. We already have more than twenty-five people ready with the cash. We just need to hand over the question paper to them. Half the amount will be paid on the spot and the remainder after the exam,' Varun added.

'What if you get caught? You will have wasted three years of your life. Worse, they may never allow you to appear for your exams again,' Garima whispered in a low tone. She was aware that everyone was taking this risk for her sake.

Varun walked closer to Garima and said, 'You know what, I had an imaginary friend when I was a kid. As I grew older I realized most of the people who claim to be your friends are imaginary. Luckily, I have got the three of you now. So now it's my turn to do something. But on a serious note, I am clueless as to what I will do if they catch me.'

They all hugged each other; no words were exchanged. Anxiety hovered in the air. The real test of life had begun already. After exchanging a few grave glances, Varun left to meet his senior.

Life comes in boxes of various sizes, holding moments that are good and bad. The contents may vary in proportion but you can't choose to escape any one of them at your convenience. An individual decides if they want to make the most of each one of the contents. No matter what our opinion, we have to accept things the way they are.

'I am fucked. I don't know how I will pass my mathematics exam tomorrow,' Varun said, pretending to be nervous in front of his senior.

'Shit happens, dude. That's the whole idiotic part of our system. It ensures women live with fear and suppresses the youth with loads of exams,' the senior cribbed as if he knew everything that went on in this world.

'I wish I was gutsy enough to get help from the lab assistant, like you did. Life would be a cakewalk,' Varun bemoaned, hoping that he would reveal something.

'Who? That Yadav? He is just a small player in all of this. Someone else is the captain. Don't get into all that. We just do it for the money. Not for clearing our exams. Sometimes if the authorities find out that the paper has been leaked they change the questions,' the senior replied.

Varun's work was done. He had got the little piece of information that he needed about the lab assistant. Bidding him goodbye, Varun went straight to the lab assistant Yadav who was busy working in the chemistry lab. Varun approached Yadav, trying to hide his nervousness. It was not the first time he was interacting with him but this time the reason was different. He feared the consequences if Yadav did a sudden U-turn and told the professors about him. But he had to take the risk. His heart was beating very fast and he heartily wished things would come to an end soon. Yadav spotted him and asked him what he was doing there.

'Actually, I wanted to ask you something. Rather, wanted some help. Senior dada is my friend,' Varun stammered.

'What help?'

'The same help that senior dada takes from you.'

'I don't know anything. Please don't disturb me,' Yadav said, pretending he was clueless.

'Please. I know it's my first time but I am ready to pay you. You are the actual authority here in college. Others are nothing compared to you. Senior dada always appreciates you. I just want tomorrow's mathematics paper. Please help me. I am not bad in academics. I have very good internal scores too. But I had an accident a few days ago and hence couldn't concentrate on my studies. Please sir, help me. I will pay you as much as you want,' Varun pleaded, trying to persuade the lab assistant.

'You think I do this for money? I don't understand your generation at all. You think you can buy anything if you have money? Go away,' Yadav shouted.

'No . . . but . . .'

Yadav gave him a long lecture on humanity, ethics and how the new generation takes everything for granted, even university rules. But as Varun was about to leave, Yadav stopped him and said, 'Beta, I don't do this usually. But you seem to be an innocent guy. You should not do such things. Just for you . . . remember, just for you I am doing this, else I would never do such a thing. It's against my ethics. But I feel for you and since you are like my kid I shall help you. Usually, I don't charge a fee but you know the university peon charges me. So you need to give me twenty thousand rupees.'

Varun smiled and agreed to his terms. He burst out laughing as soon as he left the lab. Yadav acting like a man of principles was the funniest thing he had ever witnessed. It was like a person who had a bhajan as his caller tune while answering his phone with a 'bol bhenchod'. Varun returned to inform everyone that he had cracked the deal and that they had to go to the university that night to execute their master plan. The next few hours would decide the fate of the four friends.

It was around 11 p.m. and as instructed by the lab assistant Yadav, all four of them waited near the Xerox shop in front of the university. They anxiously looked from side to side as they stood by the road. Yadav was expected any time now.

The wait didn't last long as within the next few minutes Yadav and another person got out of an autorickshaw. Both men shot Varun an annoyed look for bringing his friends along.

'You were supposed to come alone,' Yadav exclaimed.

'You too,' Varun said, looking at the unknown person accompanying him.

'He is my partner.'

'They are my friends,' Varun said in a firm voice to hide his nervousness.

Clueless as to who the other person was, Varun and the gang followed Yadav and him into a small lane that had stationery shops. The strange man ordered everyone to enter one of the shops and be seated. No one asked any questions; they were pretty scared anyway.

'Aren't we supposed to go inside the university?' asked Varun finally.

'Have patience. You can always leave if you don't like it here,' Yadav declared.

With no other option, they stayed put in their seats for the next thirty minutes looking at each other's faces. Suddenly, Yadav's partner entered the Xerox shop along with another man who introduced himself as the owner of the shop. It was evident that even the owner of the shop was involved in the racket. Yadav's partner gave the shopkeeper two thousand-rupee notes. He then gestured to them to follow him and they started walking towards the university gates. The security guard, whose job it was to look out for suspicious activities, saluted the owner of the shop and let everyone inside without any questions. As they walked towards the sciences building, Varun and the others started to sweat in fear. The passage was completely dark and even the slightest sound made them feel like someone was watching them and would expose the racket.

Varun looked towards Malvika who signalled that this was dangerous. But Varun was determined to save Garima. As they reached the BSc department, they came upon a peon who sat on a chair, smoking a cigarette.

'Singh hai upar?' the store owner asked.

He nodded and the man went upstairs. The peon didn't ask a single question but continued smoking, staring suspiciously at Varun and the girls. Yadav and his partner were very relaxed, as if they were out for an evening walk. This was probably a routine thing for them. However, Varun and the girls were literally shaking with fear. After finishing his cigarette, the peon went upstairs.

'Just wait here,' Yadav ordered Varun and he too went upstairs.

His partner sat on the peon's chair. Garima took Varun aside and whispered, 'At any point, if you think that we are being trapped or feel uncomfortable, just back out. We will find another way. But I don't want to put the rest of our lives at stake. Don't think about me. Whenever you feel like backing out, just inform me. We will all support your decision and run away in time. It's still our choice as we are the ones paying them. Just be alert and remember what I am saying.'

Varun just nodded and didn't utter a word. The next moment Yadav's partner got a call on his cell phone. It was Yadav, giving him the green signal to send Varun up while his partner was to wait downstairs with the girls and monitor the surroundings and alert them of anything suspicious.

'I am not leaving these girls alone here. I don't even know you. How can I just leave them here with you?' Varun seemed a little disturbed.

'I am not going to rape them, you dumbass. Himmat nahin hain toh kaand kyu karte ho?' he said, glaring angrily at Varun.

Varun apologized as things would have gone haywire had he argued with him. Thus avoiding complications, he did as he was told to. He started walking towards the staircase to the first floor where Yadav and the owner of the shop were waiting for him. He turned back once to look at the girls who were equally nervous and tense. Malvika's eyes pleaded with him to come back as this was starting to look like a deathtrap laid out for them. Garima had already voiced her concerns, Ahana looked shaky as well. Terror had subsumed their souls completely. Varun was scared of the sound of his own footsteps as he climbed the stairs.

Am I a criminal? Suddenly I have started to doubt myself. But I can do anything for my friends. I have never received such unconditional love. Now I don't want to lose them. I have heard that a mother forgives her son even if he is a criminal. I hope my mom forgives me. I know I am hurting her if she is watching from above, but Mom, you know why I'm doing this. I feel so confused but do I have a choice? I didn't have one earlier too and hence here I am. I wonder who the captain is—the one senior dada mentioned. Is it the shop owner? Or Mr Singh? His thoughts haunted Varun as he finally reached the floor where everyone was waiting for him.

'This is Mr Singh, the peon of the examination department. Pay him the entire amount,' said Yadav.

'First give me the question paper.'

Mr Singh nodded and told everyone to follow him. They entered a locked office to which he had the keys. The sealed copies of next day's question paper were kept in an envelope inside a drawer.

Now I understand that it's not really easy to walk on the wrong path, thought Varun. *Walking on the right path may be more difficult but at least you have your peace of mind. Here, every minute I feel like someone is watching me and will trap me. Why am I thinking so much now that it's already half done? I think I should let things happen. Or should I stop this? But stop it now? What if the captain comes? Or is he already here? No . . . let it happen. I am not a criminal, just an innocent guy trapped in the game of life.*

Varun thought of backing out at the last minute. 'Actually, sir . . . I don't want to—'

Before Varun could complete his sentence, Mr Singh interrupted him and said in a heavy tone, 'I hope you know who we are.'

It was not safe to stay there for long but they had to settle the issue. The girls were getting restless with every passing minute. Mr Singh opened the sealed envelope with the exam paper and gave it to Yadav.

'You can get a Xerox copy of this from his shop.' Mr Singh pointed towards the shop owner.

'Quick. We have to go back as well.'

The shop owner was about to leave when Varun insisted on taking a photograph of the question paper. He was not keen on going to the shop and prolonging the process. It added an unnecessary risk. He instead took photographs of the paper using his cell phone camera. After checking that the photographs were clear, he handed over the entire amount to Yadav and left the place in a hurry.

The girls were relieved when they saw Varun coming down the stairs. He nodded, indicating that the work was done. Just as they were about to leave, Yadav's partner stopped them to check with Yadav if they were allowed to go. Once he got the go-ahead, he accompanied them to the gate and told them to leave swiftly in case anyone saw them.

The most valuable lessons in life cannot be taught; they must be experienced and learnt. Varun had experienced a nightmare and had escaped before being caught. They screamed in joy on the drive back to Navi Mumbai. Varun sent the photos of the question paper to everyone who had paid him half the money. The work was half done. All of them were waiting to see if the actual question paper tallied with the one that they had. Only then would they be paid the other half of the money. Varun prayed everything would go well. He knew sometimes the question paper was changed at the last moment. If that should happen, they would have to return the money taken from the students and it would bring them back to square one. Thus all hopes were on the questions that would appear in the paper rather than answering them correctly.

'Never before in my life have I been so curious and impatient to see the question paper,' Varun said as he got ready to leave for college the next day.

Malvika and Garima were studying for their exams while Ahana was preparing for a project submission. But they could hardly concentrate.

'Please inform us before you start your exam,' Garima called out as Varun closed the door behind him and left.

He wanted to reach college early to make sure that everything was under control. He met a few students to whom he had sent the paper last night and told them not to worry. Varun took his hall ticket and entered the examination centre. Those few minutes seemed like the longest of his life. He was just praying for things to go well.

When I want to do some last-minute revision, the supervisor hounds me to put my bag outside and take the question paper. Today when I am sitting here for so long, the bastard does not even bother to look at me, he thought.

The next moment he was called to collect the question paper. Without blinking, he checked all the questions at one go.

Fuck! Fuck! Fuck! Goodness! When he saw no one looking, he immediately sent a message to Malvika. He then made an excuse that he had forgotten his pen and went outside to leave his mobile in his bag as cell phones were not allowed inside the examination hall.

He wrote just two words in the message—Mission accomplished!

After that everything went as per plan. Once they got all the money, Garima handed it over to the blackmailer. She was just asked to leave the bag outside a nearby coffee shop and go back home without looking. She didn't tell anyone who he was. It was a little absurd on her part but Varun had assumed it was Sid and wanted to teach him a lesson for sure. They were the kind of friends who wouldn't be able to attend each other's funeral if any one of them were to be murdered because they would be in prison for killing the murderer. Varun thought that Garima was keeping the identity of the blackmailer a secret from him to avoid a showdown. His priority was bringing a smile back on Garima's face and he was successful in doing so. Garima felt relieved that day. Malvika and Ahana were happy now that Garima was smiling and things were back to normal.

There is a small difference between hiding something and lying. Garima was not lying. She was just hiding information because she wanted to keep the bad memories to herself. She knew where to draw the line. Sometimes we have friends with whom our souls are very closely connected. We know that wherever we are in our lives, we will remain friends. Even if we do not see each other for years, we will be able to pick up from where we left off. Such was the bond they shared.

Karma Is a Sweet Bitch

We love certain people not because they give us what we need, but because they give us what we never felt we needed because we couldn't imagine such a thing to exist. Ahana and Garima loved each other and enjoyed each other's company for the same reason. Ahana would have done anything for Garima and Garima too would have crossed the line for her friend. They were out for an evening walk after a routine check-up at the hospital. Ahana was trying to pep Garima up, telling her to relax and erase the memory of the past few days from her life.

'C'mon, smile. There are so many hot guys out here.' Ahana winked at Garima.

'I am fine now.'

'Did you confirm that the guy deleted the videos and photographs?' Ahana questioned with concern.

'Yes. I did. I even formatted his phone,' Garima lied.

'Do you mind talking about it now?' Ahana questioned.

'I think I am comfortable enough with all of you now. I assure you that after our exams, I will tell you the entire story. Trust me,' Garima answered.

'I will be waiting to hear it. Also, it won't affect our relationship even a bit. I love you, bitch.' Ahana hugged her.

'Can I ask you something?' Garima paused and added, 'Do you think Sid was the right guy for you?'

Ahana had not expected such a question from Garima. She said it was just a passing affair and she never took it seriously.

'I liked his company and thought of just giving it a shot. It didn't work out and I moved on. I am not the kind of a person who thinks that if you love someone you should let them go and if your love is true they will come back. I believe if they keep coming back, it's not love, it's for fulfilling of their own selfish needs.' She laughed.

Ahana's relationship with her dad had shaped her attitude all these years and made her mentally strong but at the same time it made her slightly cold-hearted and as a result she never took her romantic relationships seriously.

'You know what, every day I wish my dad would call me and inquire about my studies and how life is progressing but he doesn't. Sometimes I feel jealous of Malvika whose dad calls her every day to check her whereabouts. There is no one who cares about me. I feel alone sometimes but I have accepted things as they are. I just want to prove myself to the world, to show them that I am not a loser and one day I will make my own name in the fashion industry.'

'It's the opposite for me. I never wanted to be with my family as somewhere I felt dejected in their company. Now after meeting you all and living here with you, I don't want to go back to them at all. I wish this phase of life would last forever. After a few years when we look back and think about our college days, we will laugh at all this madness. Each crazy memory will bring a big smile to our faces. All of you, your company has changed my outlook towards life. I am still a confused soul but much better than before. And yes, I will tell you my complete story after these exams,' Garima promised.

A lot of people end up unhappy because they make permanent decisions based on temporary emotions. However, Ahana was not one of them. She lived for the moment and searched for happiness in it. Garima too had decided to open up to her friends and tell them of the haunting memories that had changed her as a person as she grew up. They were so lost in conversation that they didn't realize it was getting late. Sometimes all you need to feel better is to spend a few minutes alone with a very close friend.

One should not worry when a girl cares too much about you; one should worry when she stops caring. Varun had no worries on that front as he had Malvika by his side who cared about him a lot. They were sitting alone in their room thinking about how life had tricked them by dealing unexpected cards on the table. They looked into each other's eyes and Varun kissed her forehead, giving her a warm hug.

'It feels as if a violent storm has just passed. I hope there are no more troubles in our lives,' Malvika whispered.

Varun kissed her earlobe and muttered, 'If you are with me, we will overcome all the troubles with ease. I just hope Garima finds the strength to move on. I still wonder about her past though.'

'I do too but she has never revealed anything to me either. She was deeply hurt. Maybe someone betrayed her love. This entire incident has traumatized her. We need to make her believe that her life is beautiful.'

Varun wanted to meet Sid just once so he could blow his head off. In all the chaos of the past weeks, he had hardly found any time to spend with Malvika. He held her close and kissed her tender lips.

'We are going to get married someday,' Malvika said, blushing.

'Of course. That will be the second best day of my life,' Varun said, running his fingers through her hair.

'What was the first?' Malvika asked in curiosity.

'The first will be when I meet your parents. Usually a girl's father always taunts her choice of a mate, as for the first time she has found someone else to live with. But I won't let that happen. I want him to treat me like a son. I have never experienced fatherly love in my life. Mothers are emotional. I know your mom is too and will love me for sure. But I will make your dad love me more than you do. That will be the best day of my life.'

'Awww. That's so sweet.'

'I know.' He laughed.

You know you are in love when you wake up and that person is your first thought, when you keep checking your phone to see if they have texted or called you while you were asleep, when you miss them even though it has not been long since you last met. But mostly, you're in love when you put their needs before your own, when their happiness is more important than your pain. When you are in love, you are ready to give it all. Just like Varun and Malvika who were completely and adorably in love.

I have reached. Waiting near the parking lot, Varun messaged his friends as he waited for them outside the college premises to collect some important notes for the second exam. As he waited, he received a message from Malvika.

Malvika: *What's up?*

Varun: *Nothing, condom on the floor and am drunk.*

Malvika: *WTF?*

Varun: *And they say I have good sense of humour. :P*

Malvika: *What will you do if I broke up with you?*

Varun: *Go back to my ex.*

Malvika: *Huh. Now I see how much you care. I am done. Go to your ex.*

Varun: *You are my ex. Once you break up with me.*

Malvika: *I love you.*

Varun: *Suddenly?*

Malvika: *Just missing you.*

Varun: *Iloveyoutoo.*

Malvika: *Something wrong with the space bar?*

Varun: *No. There's just no space for me to love anyone else.*

Suddenly, Varun's smile vanished as he saw some cops walking towards him. For a minute, he thought that the game was over. Everything that had happened in the past few days flashed before his eyes and he started thinking of excuses for what he had done. He panicked and thought of running away but that would have made them suspicious. He stood there like a statue. The cops came up to him and asked, 'Where is the principal's office?'

'Upstairs, it's on the first floor. But today there are no classes. So he might not be in his office. What happened?' Varun stammered.

'Are you from the BSc class?'

Varun nodded. The cops told him that they had received a complaint from a student who claimed that he got the BSc maths question paper on WhatsApp and Facebook early on the morning of the exam. They also told him that they had lodged a complaint after seeing the photographs and were looking into this matter seriously. Varun had not expected this even in his worst nightmare. All of a sudden, he imagined himself behind bars and started shivering with fear. He messaged Malvika and the others about this. Everyone was shocked. No one could figure out what their next move should be. It would not be a difficult task for the cops to get a hold of them once they started their investigation.

Varun thought for a while and went looking for Yadav, the lab assistant. He confessed to him that he had leaked the paper to a few students before the exam to get some money and now the cops were investigating. Yadav too was terrified on hearing this. No one had ever found out about this scam before.

'Please do something. I don't want to end up behind bars,' Varun pleaded.

'How could you do that? Because of your foolishness I will go to jail. Leave me alone for now,' Yadav screamed.

This was the first time that Varun was dealing with such a problem and hence was completely clueless. He called all the students to whom he had sold the paper but everyone denied telling the cops or even sharing it with someone else. Varun was sure that it was uploaded by one of them as the cops had clearly mentioned that the message was sent by someone from this college. He felt guilty for not having taken the necessary precautions so no one could upload it on social media platforms. But was it really possible to stop the information from being uploaded on social media sites once it was already leaked? There was no point in thinking what could have been done. They were screwed. He went back home to a nervous bunch of friends.

'Fuck, dude, we shouldn't have done it,' Malvika cried.

'Now what?' Garima questioned in a tense voice.

'I have no idea. If we get caught, I will take all the blame. I shouldn't have suggested this idea at all,' Varun exclaimed.

'We are all equally at fault. Don't blame yourself,' Ahana stated.

'Instead of playing the blame game, we should find a solution,' Malvika suggested.

'We are not professional criminals. We can't use our brains to devise solutions to such troubles. There is no way out. It's just a wait-and-watch game now until we get arrested.' Varun sighed.

The consequences of the choices you make can change your life in the blink of an eye. Hence one should think a thousand times before doing something wrong because sometimes it can't be undone. Varun sat there, distraught about the entire scenario. They had managed to solve one problem only to have another waiting for them. However, this time there was no escape. With each passing hour, the tension reached new levels. The stress was unbearable but they could do absolutely nothing about it. Varun was not able to concentrate and hence didn't perform well in the next couple of papers. It's not easy to live a normal life once you have committed a crime. The guilt haunts you and that's exactly what was happening to Varun. Three papers were over and except the first one, he was sure to flunk the others. You can reappear for your college exams if you flunk, but life doesn't give you a second chance if you flunk the test of survival.

The police investigation was being carried out with full force and within a few days they had managed to join several threads connected to the case. The investigators got a tip that a certain Mr Rao, who was Yadav's partner and worked as a peon at a private coaching class at Dadar, had been selling the leaked papers to the students. Rao was picked up and his interrogation revealed that the papers reached him through the Xerox shop owner Sharma, the university peon Kamble and Singh, who worked as a peon in the university examination department where the question papers were kept. Meanwhile, the police was also trying to determine the identity of the WhatsApp user who first distributed the question paper. It was a matter of time now before the cops caught hold of the lab assistant Yadav and then Varun and the group. It was already too late for Varun, Malvika, Ahana and Garima.

Do Not Touch Me

Each day I live, the pain consumes
What little stability I have bloomed
Like walking in a cloud of fog
Falling down, sinking into smog

Life just seems grim
I think on a whim
Interest lost in everything I do
But what a life, who really knew?
Depressed to a fault, that's all I see
Prison just seems like the only way for me
A waste of time, I feel I am
But that's its nature, a full mind jam

I try and try to ease the pain
A fallen effort with no gain
Thoughts begin to eat away
Makes me want to end it today

Uncomfortable around others because of the way I feel
I pray and wish all of this wasn't real
Life just seems more like a prison
Caged, alone, an outrage risen

No one could ever understand
Why I would want my death sooner than planned
It's not something I want for me
But to end my suffering this is what has to be

Varun sat alone in his room writing his thoughts in his personal diary. He had come to believe that all was lost and the end was near. That's when Ahana entered his room and told him that Sid had called her and wanted to meet. Varun told Ahana to call Sid home.

'Are you sure?' she asked to confirm.

'Yes. I want to teach that bastard a lesson. This entire episode started because of him and now I will put a full stop to it,' Varun said furiously.

Malvika tried to convince Varun to let Ahana meet him alone but he was not ready to back off. He screamed at everyone, including Garima, ordering them to stay away and let him handle the situation his way.

'Just make sure he doesn't create a scene in the society. People already say all sorts of things behind our backs,' Ahana whispered to Malvika.

Malvika assured her that she would keep Varun in check. She told Garima not to worry as there was panic written all over her face. Ahana finally messaged Sid to come over and he replied saying he would reach within the next hour. It's hard to resist the urge to say 'Fuck you' to someone who really deserves it. Varun had a similar urge but refrained from saying anything.

The bell rang and everyone looked at Varun as he got up to open the door. The moment Sid entered the room, Varun punched him in the face and knocked him down to the floor with a brutal kick. Varun continued smashing his face, punch after punch, not giving Sid an opportunity to fight back. Each punch left a bruise on his face.

'Son of a bitch. I will kill you. How dare you do this? Because of you our lives are at stake. Who gave you the right to play with our lives? You think extorting all that money from us makes you a cool dude?' Varun screamed at the top of his voice.

Sid tried to catch his breath and said, 'I have no idea what you're talking about.'

'Stop these fucking lies. Don't try to act innocent in front of Ahana.'

'Trust me. Why should I lie? I am not here to patch up with Ahana. I just came to inquire about Garima's health.'

'Then why did you blackmail Garima for money with the MMS and the nude photos?' Ahana questioned, looking confused.

'What? I didn't! I don't know anything about any nude pictures or MMS. I just took a short video where I was kissing Garima in the washroom of that lounge when she was drunk out of her senses. The one I sent to all of you. I didn't take anything else apart from that and a few photographs. I just wanted to threaten her as Ahana was not responding to my calls or messages. I was hurt and it was all because of Garima. She was the one who took photos and videos of me with that girl. I wanted to teach her a similar lesson. Hence, I too made a video but I never circulated it or blackmailed her.'

'You didn't circulate it or blackmail her?' Malvika repeated in a serious tone.

'No . . . I mean . . . okay, I showed it to the gym manager just to show off but apart from that I never blackmailed anyone. In fact, Garima's uncle met me and threatened to put me behind bars after that incident. I never even texted you or anyone related to you,' Sid said, looking at Ahana.

'Garima's uncle?' Varun asked.

Garima was sitting in a corner of the room nervously watching all that was going on.

'Yes. Her uncle threatened me when he found out that Garima had attempted suicide because of the video that I took of us kissing. The gym manager told him as such when he came to the gym to inquire about Garima. Trust me, I never thought Garima would take such a harsh step. I felt really guilty when I found out. I wanted to meet all of you but Garima's uncle warned me not to. I handed over all the clips and photographs to him that day. I have nothing with me. How could I blackmail her?'

'So what brings you here now?'

'I was feeling guilty and the other day I saw Ahana and Garima leaving the hospital. I couldn't stop myself and after a lot of hesitation I messaged Ahana to meet me first. I guessed that Garima's uncle would have left by now.'

Varun could not believe what Sid was saying. Not once had Garima mentioned her uncle. Ahana and Malvika too were left stunned. Garima had not lied but had delayed in confessing the truth. She was apprehensive about discussing her past and was still petrified of her tormentor. However, she had decided to reveal the truth after the exams. Little did she know it would come out in this way.

'What's all this? Care to explain?' Varun seemed annoyed.

'I was about to tell you guys . . . whatever Sid is saying is true . . . Sid was not the one who called me for the money. It was . . . my uncle,' Garima stammered.

Her entire body started shivering the moment she took the name. Malvika went close to her and held her hand.

'I want to know everything. Now.' Varun ignored the fear in Garima's eyes.

'Can I have a glass of water?' Garima pleaded.

Her head started hurting. The traumatic episode flashed before her eyes. She had avoided the truth for so long. It was pointless to discuss it again after her mom kept shushing her and shoving the truth under the carpet. But today, she had to face the facts.

'I was ten years old . . . We lived in a joint family. He would bring chocolates for me. Imported ones too as he travelled to Mumbai a lot. He made me sit on his lap and played with me. Everyone thought he cared for me. He "cared for me" even more when we were alone, in the bathroom. He would make me sit on his lap there too. I would scream but he kept his hand on my mouth so that my screams were inaudible. It would hurt a lot.

'"Done . . . done . . . done. You are so sexy, my puppy," he would say.

'No one noticed and he too told me not to tell anyone. But after gathering my courage I revealed everything to my mom. She thought I was lying. My own mother ignored my pain. My first memories as a child are of being molested repeatedly. This has affected every aspect of my life. This darkness, which is the only way I can describe it, has followed me like a fog, but at times it intensified and overwhelmed me, usually triggered by a particular situation.

'He continued hurting me until I left home for high school. One night before I left, he made me sit on his lap and did things to me which no child should endure at that tender age.

'That's all I can remember apart from my physical pain. I remember spending hours playing Scrabble alone; my world consisted of a box of cold, plastic blocks. It's the same thing I do now, but instead of Scrabble, I surf the web or read or watch a cricket match. Most of my life has been spent feeling dead inside, waiting for my body to catch up. At times while growing up I would feel a huge rage, but I never connected this to what had happened until puberty. I was able to keep the darkness away for a few hours at a time by doing things that required intense concentration, but it would always come back. I feel like I'm trapped in a contaminated body that no amount of washing will clean.

'Three to four nights a week I have nightmares about what happened. It makes me avoid sleep and I am constantly tired, because sleeping with what feels like hours of nightmares is not restful. I wake up sweating and furious. I'm reminded every morning of what was done to me and the control it has over my life. When my uncle found out about my suicide attempt from the message Malvika left on voicemail at my home, he came to Mumbai. My parents were not in town and hence they didn't know something like this had happened. My uncle deleted the message and never told them. Anyway, I don't want them to know, as they never supported me though I was their own child. I was too embarrassed to tell my dad and when my mom didn't support me, I lost all confidence in them.

'After coming to Mumbai, my uncle met Sid and warned him to stay away. Sid obeyed but my uncle instead of consoling me started blackmailing me. I knew instantly that it was my uncle when I received the call. He gave me two choices. Either sleep with him or pay him the money. He said he knew that I couldn't pay him so I'd better cooperate or he would expose me. I was terrified and convinced you all to agree to pay the money. I hope now I have justified my actions.'

No one uttered a word as she continued.

'I've never been able to stop thinking about what happened to me and this hampered my social interactions. I walked around viewing the world from a distance. I wondered what it would be like to talk to other people without what happened being constantly on my mind, and

I wondered if other people had similar experiences that they were better able to mask.

'Alcohol provided a way to ignore the realities of my situation. It was easy to spend the night drinking in my room secretly, being able to forget that I had no future to look forward to. I never liked what alcohol did to me but it was better than facing my existence honestly. I haven't touched alcohol or any other drug in the last few years until that night when Sid took the advantage of the situation.

'I didn't realize how deep a hold the darkness had on me and my life until my first relationship in high school. I stupidly assumed that no matter how the darkness affected me personally, my romantic relationships would somehow be separate and protected. Growing up I viewed my future relationships as a possible escape from this thing that haunts me every day but I began to realize how entangled it was with every aspect of my life and how it is never going to release me. The relationship started out fine but as we got closer emotionally the darkness would return. Every night it'd be me, him and the darkness in a fearful threesome. It made me hate being touched. I realized that I would never be able to give him, or anyone, all of me. I realized that the darkness would never allow me to be in a relationship. I will never get to feel the warmth of someone's arms, the comfort of their hands around me. I will never know what uncontaminated intimacy is like. I will never have an exclusive bond with someone, someone who can be the recipient of all the love I have to give. I think I would have made a good mom.

'I've spent my life hurting people. I've never told anyone about what happened to me, ever, for obvious reasons. It took me a while to realize that no matter how close you are to someone or how much they claim to love you, people simply cannot keep secrets. The more harmful the secret, the juicier the gossip and the more likely you are to be betrayed. People don't care about their word or what they've promised, they just do whatever the fuck they want and justify it later. It feels incredibly lonely to realize you can never share something with someone and have it be just between the two of you. I don't blame anyone in particular; I guess it's just how people are. So even if I were able to trust someone, I probably would not tell them what happened to me. That was the only reason I never revealed my past to all of you. Ahana asked me the other day and I said that I would after the exams. Malvika had asked me so many times in the past but I always avoided telling her. Being abused has defined me as a person and shaped me as a human being and it has made me the way I am and there's nothing I can do to escape it.

'But trust me, I actually started living when I met all of you. I never enjoyed life before you entered my life. I just felt fundamentally broken, almost non-human. But life is beautiful. I accepted that when Malvika made me realize what true friends are like. Ahana protected me like a sister and Varun, you were with me whenever I needed you. I never had to express my needs to you.

'You may wonder why I don't just talk to a professional about this. I have no interest in talking about being molested as a child, both because I know it wouldn't help and because I have no confidence it will remain secret. I know the legal and practical implications of all this. I was scared everything would be made public and I'd be forced to live in a world where people would know how fucked up I am. And yes, I realize this indicates that I have severe trust issues, but they're based on a large number of experiences with people who have shown a profound disrespect for their word and the privacy of others.

'When Sid sent me the clips, I tried to end my life. People say suicide is selfish. I think it's selfish to ask people to continue living painful and miserable lives. Suicide may be a permanent solution to a temporary problem, but it's also a permanent solution to a seventeen-year-old problem that grows more intense and overwhelming every day. I know many people have it worse than I do, and maybe I'm just not a strong person, but I really did try to deal with this. I've tried to deal with this every day for the past seventeen years and I just couldn't fucking take it any more. But the way you pampered me after my return from hospital helped me regain some of my confidence. Even before that, my confidence was boosted when I spent memorable times with all of you. I consider the three of you as my family and I mean it. I am really grateful that you agreed to help me and take such a big risk. When we got the money, I called my uncle and told him that I am coming. He thought I had given up and was agreeing to sleep with him. He even booked a room in a fancy hotel where he asked me to meet him. I didn't tell him that I had the money until I reached there. I threw the money on his face and slapped him. The slap was not as hard as the permanent scars he has left on my soul but was enough to make him realize I am not weak any more. Don't worry; I will take all the blame if the police find us guilty.'

Varun apologized for being arrogant while Ahana and Malvika comforted Garima and told her all would be okay. Though they were worried about the cops, their attention was focused on Garima. We experience pain to know relief, sadness to know joy, love to know loss, fear to know courage and mistakes to know our strength. Their strength was their togetherness.

For One Last Time

You can twist and bend the truth as much as you want, but eventually it'll all come out. Stress was eating away at the four of them every minute of their lives. How were they to cope with what was happening? They had no clue at all. After Garima's confession, they were very disturbed and felt extremely sorry for her. To relieve the stress, they went to the fast food centre in Sector 19, Sea Woods. And though it's easy to try and 'move on', it's extremely tough to divert your mind from a depressing situation.

'I am sorry, Garima; I thought you'd lied to us,' Varun muttered.

'It's okay. You've all done so much for me. I couldn't expect more,' Garima said, trying to smile.

'The primary question still remains—how are we supposed to get out of this trap? Isn't there a way out?' Ahana asked.

'There is one solution. But I am not too keen on it,' Varun opened up.

'What's that?'

'My dad. He is a retired army man. I am sure he can help us but I'd rather go to jail than take his help,' Varun said.

'Oh Varun, just put your ego aside,' Ahana mumbled.

'You are still so adamant. I told you to forgive him. He must have had his reasons for doing what he did,' Malvika whispered, holding his hand.

'You think it can work? Everyone except our lab assistant is under interrogation. Once the police get hold of him, we are an easy catch. How can your dad help in this case?' Garima asked nervously.

'I don't know. I remember my senior saying don't get into all this. Yadav is just a small player. The real captain is someone else.'

Varun wished he had taken the advice seriously and stayed away. The hardest thing is knowing that you are falling apart . . . and realizing that you have lost the thing that holds you together!

Life, fortune and mishaps are unpredictable; nobody knows what surprises tomorrow will bring. Thus some words are better said early and some chances taken soon. Despite Varun's objection, Malvika convinced Ahana and Garima to consult his dad about a solution. Ahana was reluctant in the beginning, fearing Varun's father would tell her dad too, but later was convinced of the plan. She knew it was better to face reality than ruin one's image in society by getting arrested. You can Photoshop your profile picture but you cannot change your image once it's messed up. Garima too agreed to the plan, though she was not sure whether it would really be of any help. They decided not to inform Varun about it until there was no other alternative.

Ahana took the initiative of calling Varun's dad but as she wanted to make sure that his dad flew down to Mumbai, she didn't tell him the real scenario. Instead she told him that Varun was seriously injured. She also requested him not to contact Varun directly or tell him that she had called as Varun was still upset with him. Varun's dad took the news seriously and immediately booked his ticket to Mumbai. Though they had disputes and continuous fights, he was Varun's father. The entire time he was worried about what had happened to Varun. It's never easy for a father to see his son in hospital. No matter how sour the relationship between them might be.

As soon as he landed in Mumbai, he called Ahana who was already at the airport to receive him along with Garima and Malvika.

'What happened to him? Is he serious?' Varun's dad asked in a shaky voice.

Ahana didn't answer his question. Instead she politely told him to get in the car. Varun's dad glanced at Malvika and Garima who were seated at the back. They greeted him with a namaste.

'Will you please tell me? I know I am not a good father. But at least I have a right to know what has happened to my son. Is he no more?' he asked, fearing the worst.

'Uncle, please don't say such things. We will tell you the whole story,' Malvika interrupted from the back seat.

Ahana too requested him to calm down and drove to Hiranandani Powai where they took him to the Saffron Spice Hotel for a heart-to-heart. Not just Varun's dad, even the girls were nervous as they knew they had called him under false pretences even though their intentions were clear.

'What will you have, Uncle?' Ahana asked.

'Why are we here? Please, will you tell me what the matter is?' Varun's dad pleaded.

With a lot of courage, Ahana explained the entire scenario—about how they had leaked the university papers and how badly they were trapped in the situation. However, she didn't say anything about Garima's uncle blackmailing her. Malvika added that all those who were included in the scandal were under interrogation and even Varun wanted him to help but didn't come forward for obvious reasons.

Varun's dad was furious on hearing this. His anger was to a certain extent expected and justified. No one dared to speak until he broke the silence.

'Today, I am not angry with you girls. I am angry with myself for not being a good father. Varun is a young man now and I know he wants to do what his heart feels, which is why he cannot understand my views on life. Yes, I wanted him to join the army so that he could learn discipline. I wanted him to be a good human. Unlike me. Nothing I have ever done has given me more joy, and rewarded me as much, than being a father to Varun. The day I found out that he was going to be born was the happiest and scariest moment of my life. You are not given a manual on how to raise a child, but I was going to do everything I could for him. But life changed after Varun's mom died. All of a sudden she left us, and it left me frustrated and depressed. The loneliness killed me from the inside. Though we have never talked about it, many a time in his childhood I would hit him, irritated by my suppressed frustration. One of those times stands out sharply in my memory. I think he was about eight. I came home more frustrated than usual. I was about to go to bed. He was throwing a ball in his room, which I had previously told him not to. I heard the crash of broken glass and ran into his room to see that he had just broken a window. I lost it and started hitting him, several times, on his face. I think that was the worst. Afterwards, he was crying and I felt terrible, but I never apologized for my cruel actions.

'Today I want him to know how sorry I am for every time I hurt him. The grief has stayed in my heart for months and years. I have often judged myself a bad father because of that episode alone though there were many more. My fault was that I failed in interacting with my son. I never sat with him and asked him what he sought from life. I never confessed why I would get angry. Of course, my actions were wrong but my intentions were not. No child deserves to be hit by a parent or anyone else. I needed to let him know how upset I felt in each situation. I should have expressed my anger, my disappointment, with words rather than my hands. But I had never learnt that from my own father. What I did to my son I had learnt from him. He used to abuse and hit me. It's terrible how abuse can get passed down from generation to generation. My greatest hope is that this terrible legacy stops with him. I know he will take time to forgive me but some day when he is a father, I think he will make a better father than I ever did. It's difficult to judge this from my actions but I love him.'

The girls were speechless and moved by his pain. They apologized for lying to him.

'We are sorry, Uncle. We didn't mean to hurt you,' Malvika cried.

'That's fine. It's not your fault, my dear. I am sorry. Anyway, let's come to the point. When is his next paper?'

'Tomorrow.'

'Oh all right. Do as I say and don't ask any questions. Call the concerned person and tell him you want to leak tomorrow's examination paper at your own risk despite the police investigation and would pay him three times the usual amount.'

'The area will be under police surveillance. How will we repeat the act? Isn't there any other way?' Ahana questioned.

'No. This is the only way. Just go with it and leave the rest to me. I will handle it my way. Nothing will happen to you guys. But it's up to you to convince Varun to repeat the whole scene tonight without revealing our plan to him.'

Ahana, Malvika and Garima agreed to do as he suggested.

'Uncle, one more thing, you can't stay at our apartment. Sorry. Varun will—'

'That's fine. I will manage.'

Ahana apologized once again as they headed towards Sea Woods. Varun's dad checked in at a nearby hotel after discussing the entire plan with the girls one last time.

Isn't it funny how some friends can become family and some family members can become strangers? It's very important to communicate in any relationship to avoid misunderstandings. Both Varun and his dad had never interacted much and that had created a huge wall between them. However, his dad was here to take a stand and break the wall. But even he was not sure if it was actually possible to save Varun and his friends from such a nasty situation.

Sometimes we see things that aren't meant to be seen
Sometimes things aren't always as they seem
Sometimes people just can't understand
Why things get out of hand.
Sometimes life just isn't fair,
And sometimes it's hard to say
Why things have to be this way.
Sometimes it's all you can do to get by,
Especially when dreams continue to die.
Sometimes it's nice to sit in the rain
Even to just relieve the pain.

We never know what's wrong without pain.
Sometimes the hardest thing and the right thing are the same.
And sometimes when people get hurt,
Even the strongest ones may need comfort.

Varun was thinking about Garima and writing about how life had treated her so cruelly even though she didn't deserve it. He believed she was one of the strongest people he had met but because she was hurt, she needed comfort.

Malvika opened the door with her keys and went inside. She had told Ahana and Garima to give her some time alone with Varun so that she could convince him of the plan. Varun was sitting on the beanbag and as Malvika came near him, he pulled her towards himself and kissed her on her neck. However, Malvika pushed him away, saying she was not in the mood.

'What's wrong? Sex helps in relieving stress.' He winked.

'There is a serious problem.'

'Now what? We are already fucked. Things can't get any worse,' Varun said.

'Something more serious than that. Garima's uncle has asked for more money. He has threatened her again. But this will be the last time.'

'What the fuck? Garima had said he had deleted the photographs. Now what?' Varun asked, furious.

'No, he had a few on a pen drive. He has sent them to Garima and asked for another two lakhs after which he will leave her alone.' Malvika sat beside Varun.

'So?'

'So what? We need to do this again. One last time.'

Varun stood up in anger. He started yelling at Malvika, telling her she had gone nuts. There was so much chaos in their lives because of that one time they had been involved in that racket and now she wanted them to repeat the same thing. He was strictly against the idea and told her to stay out of it as well. But she didn't give up. She started using the age-old method of emotional blackmail.

'Baby, please, just for my sake if nothing else. You trust me, right? Do you think I would ever take a wrong decision? Please show some trust in me. I have thought this over.'

Malvika knew the trick would work and continued to convince him in a seductive tone.

'We will be screwed. I am telling you. Everyone is under interrogation. The police are yet to get hold of Yadav, the lab assistant. Everyone else is being interrogated,' Varun pleaded.

'This shows you don't trust me. I mean nothing to you.' Malvika pretended to cry.

'My princess, it's not like that. But it's risky. Anyway, I will do it for you. Where are Ahana and Garima?'

Sometimes love makes you do things you never intended to, like agreeing to watch *P.S. I Love You* over *The Fast and the Furious*. Varun finally gave in. Malvika told him to lure Yadav by telling him that they would give him three times the amount they paid last time.

Malvika immediately sent a message to Ahana and Garima: *The work is done. You both can come home. Varun has been convinced.*

When the girls came back, Varun asked if Garima was all right.

'I hope Malvika told you what has happened,' she said.

'Ya, she did but Garima, you told us that the photos were—'

Ahana interrupted Varun and requested him not to ask any further questions as Garima was already completely broken. Varun obeyed and prepared to leave for college to meet the lab assistant. He entered the lab on shaky legs. Somehow with some leftover courage he patted Yadav on the back. Yadav turned to see Varun and panicked.

'What are you doing here? Go away. Somebody will see us together. I request you not to be here at this time. Please, please leave,' Yadav pleaded.

'I . . . want to . . . You know what I mean. Actually, the thing is . . .' Varun stammered, trying to get the words out.

'Speak quickly and for God's sake, leave.'

'I am ready to pay you three times the amount, but I want tomorrow's paper. Trust me; I will take all the blame if something happens. I assure you that you won't come under the spotlight. I will be solely responsible for this. I can give it to you in writing. I don't know how you will do it without your partners but it's your call. I am ready if you are,' Varun blurted out, still afraid.

'What you're asking of me is suicidal.'

'Nothing will happen to you. This is my responsibility.' Varun tried to convince him.

Yadav made a call to confirm if it was possible to carry out the same transaction. Once he got an affirmative response, he agreed and told Varun to be at the same place and same time.

The deal was all set. Varun wondered whom Yadav was consulting on phone. Was it the captain? The mastermind behind everything? Anyway, he didn't care. Ahana, Garima and Malvika were playing along with the plan Varun's dad had suggested. Varun had blind trust in Malvika and loved her too much to refuse. The lab assistant agreed as he was lured by the promise of more money. Each one was in it for their own reasons. Varun's dad was the mastermind behind this and he too was playing for the sake of his son. No one knew the end game except Varun's dad but everyone had agreed to play hoping that it was the last time they would have to!

It was around 11 p.m. and just as before, all four of them were waiting near the Xerox shop. The shop though was closed as the owner was under interrogation. Varun was nervous that the cops would appear out of nowhere all of a sudden. Ahana, Garima and Malvika were trying to spot Varun's dad but he was nowhere to be seen. They had taken this step under his guidance. But they hadn't received a call or further instructions from him, though Ahana had informed him of the time and place. She kept looking at her mobile screen but it showed nothing except her wallpaper. She even tried calling him discreetly but there was no response.

An autorickshaw pulled up to the shop and Yadav, the lab assistant, got off alone this time. 'Come along with me,' he ordered.

Varun started walking towards the lane that Yadav had directed them to the last time. However, Yadav stopped him and told him to just follow. This time, he took them directly to the university gate.

Is it a different plan altogether? Or does the plan change every time? Varun wondered.

The giant door was not locked this time. The security guard too was missing. Varun wanted to back out but Malvika, seeing the nervousness on his face, held his hand. She once again assured him that everything would be all right even though she was clueless about what was going to happen.

The peon on the chair from the last time was missing too. Varun felt there was something odd about it all. If it was so easy this time, why was it so difficult the last time around, he thought. Yadav, like the last time, went upstairs, telling all of them to wait.

'I think we should leave. I feel there is something horribly wrong. I sense something fishy. Let's go back,' Varun stammered.

Ahana kept trying to spot Varun's dad but she couldn't. Garima and Malvika didn't react and stood still. The next moment, Varun got a call from Yadav, asking him to come upstairs alone.

'All of you will wait here?' Varun asked the girls nervously.

They nodded in agreement and Varun started walking upstairs. Yadav was waiting for him and as he reached, took him into the office where the exam papers were kept.

'He is inside, doing what he has to. We will wait here,' Yadav stated.

Varun stood as ordered by Yadav. *Who is this 'he'?* Varun thought. *The captain? Are they trying to trap me?*

There was pin-drop silence and not even the slightest sliver of light lit the corridor. All Varun could make out was a dim light inside the office. Varun didn't dare speak; his heart was in his mouth. He was worried someone was keeping an eye on them. He tried to shrug the thought off.

For a few minutes, there was no movement. Everything was at a complete standstill. Suddenly, a few people came upstairs with torches in their hands. Varun's heart skipped a beat and both he and Yadav were completely terrified. Varun closed his eyes for a moment, as he was sure it was over. They had been exposed!

Varun heard voices in the low light. Suddenly the lights were switched on and there they stood in front of him—the cops.

'Don't move. There is no escape. You are all under arrest.'

Varun immediately raised his hands, taking a nervous breath. Yadav tried to run but couldn't and was held firmly by a couple of policemen. Varun had sensed something fishy and knew he should have backed out at that moment. He pleaded with the cops but in vain. He was worried about the girls who were waiting downstairs. He remembered Malvika telling him to trust her. He couldn't figure out what she'd been thinking and cursed his fate. They had gambled and lost. When you're least expecting karma to find you, the sweet bitch installs a GPS!

Thinking Back, Looking Forward…

There are no shortcuts in life and though he was taught this lesson right from childhood, Varun truly realized the meaning that day. He stood there without speaking a word. He wanted to call Malvika to know if the girls were all right. But the cops were holding him firmly. There were policemen looking into every corner to collect all evidence of the crime. The senior inspector walked towards the office where the lights were still switched off. The person was inside hiding, but he would not remain hidden for long. The senior inspector nabbed him as soon as he opened the door. As the man resisted, the inspector slapped him hard and knocked him down. He pulled him up by his collar and once again gave him a tight slap.

'So you are the captain. People like you have made a business out of our education system. I may not be a professor but I will teach you the lesson of a lifetime,' the inspector yelled.

He looked at Varun and asked, 'Is he a professor in your college?'

Varun looked at him closely and nodded. 'Professor Shinde!' he exclaimed.

'Professor Shinde, your game is now over,' said the inspector as he handcuffed him.

The other cops followed, pulling Varun along. Varun felt like a criminal as he was dragged down the stairs forcefully. However, the thing he couldn't quite understand was how the inspector knew that the professor was the captain and the kingpin of the entire racket. What he saw downstairs gave him the biggest shock of his life. His trust shattered as he saw his dad was standing along with Ahana, Malvika and Garima.

'You have decided to make my life hell, right? I ran away to live but you managed to interfere with my life here too. What is your problem in life? When will you stop running after me?' Varun screamed at his dad.

'My problem is that . . . you are my son. And I love you,' Varun's dad said in a heavy voice.

Varun gave a sarcastic smile and said, 'Son . . . love . . . do you even know the meaning of these words? Please go away. You wanted to see me behind bars, your wish has been granted. Now go away.'

'Inspector, let him go,' Varun's dad ordered.

Varun was surprised and kept staring at his dad. He couldn't understand what was going on. He couldn't figure out whether his dad was here to arrest him or to save him from this mess. His doubts were cleared when Ahana broke the silence.

'Varun, we are sorry,' she said. 'We called your dad to Mumbai. Despite your objections, we revealed the entire truth to him. That was the only way we could have been saved. Nobody would have believed us otherwise.'

Malvika held Varun's hand and explained that his dad was here to help them and not to stand against them.

'Remember, I told you, your dad loves you.'

She looked in his eyes and her expression told him that she was not wrong at all. She told him of their entire plan that they'd kept hidden from him.

She revealed that when Varun thought of backing out the first time, Singh had introduced him to the captain but, as the transaction happened in the dark, he couldn't figure out who he was. The captain sought an opportunity to earn some money and told him he had to leak the papers or else he would expose everyone. He forced them to circulate the papers against their will so he could get paid.

'When we told your dad everything that had actually happened, he suggested repeating this entire act as it was the only way to get hold of the professor since we didn't have any strong proof against him. We didn't even know for sure if the captain was Professor Shinde. He would have escaped very easily. Hence we convinced you to do it one more time. We didn't do it for money.' Garima smiled.

The senior inspector slapped the professor again and asked him what made him do such an unethical thing. The professor, ashamed of his act, sobbed and revealed his side of the story.

'I got carried away. The day Yadav told me that a student wanted to leak a question paper I thought I could earn some money. I had done it before and had contacts in the university. I am so sorry. I am a senior professor. I see so many professors who take private tuitions and then pass their students in the exams. I never took private tuitions and hence thought of this method to earn an extra income. Yes, I was at fault. I may be a criminal but I have two daughters. They are yet to get married. I wanted to find them suitable matches and host grand weddings for them, which was not possible with my salary. Thus, I grabbed the opportunity to make a quick buck.

'I told Yadav to bring the student to the university. My accomplices were the Xerox shop owner Sharma, Yadav's partner Rao, the university peon Kamble and Singh who was the examinations department peon. We thought nobody would doubt the Xerox shop owner who brought us many clients. The students knew that he was the man to contact. Singh and Kamble used to help us open the sealed university papers. I thought, even if the police found out, Varun would be caught and no one would reach me. The next day I got the entire amount and that was that. Today when, Yadav told me that Varun was willing to pay three times the amount, I couldn't resist. How was I to know it was a trap?'

The senior inspector handcuffed him and said, 'You underestimate the police. Instead of thinking about a grand wedding for your daughter and spending lakhs of rupees on it, it would have been better if you had spent money on their education. They would have taught you what's wrong and what's right. Our education system doesn't need a professor like you who traps students and seeks to profit off them. You are under arrest.'

The police told Malvika, Varun, and Ahana that they needed to come to the police station to make a statement.

'Thank you, inspector, for your cooperation,' said Varun's dad, shaking his hand.

'I should thank you, sir. Indeed, the Indian army never retires. Thank you for your cooperation. But yes, your son and his friends are involved in this scandal. We are not arresting them as they have helped us and are our witnesses in this case. I won't file a case against them but only on the promise that they won't ever repeat this. Varun, you should thank your dad. Not everyone is lucky to get such a cooperative father.'

The police left the spot with Yadav and Professor Shinde in tow. Varun was speechless and couldn't make eye contact with anyone. The best feeling in the world is knowing that your family and friends love you just the way you are and wouldn't have you any other way. Varun's dad loved him and had supported him when he needed it the most. Malvika was his pillar of strength. Things were finally going to come to a close.

'I am sorry . . . for running away like that,' said Varun to his father. 'I don't really know where to start. I have so much to say but I don't know where to begin. You knew I was in trouble and I needed you. You knew that your presence could help me get out of this trouble.' He was very emotional.

'You are not bad,' said his dad. 'You are just too young to understand what's right and what's wrong. They are nice . . . your friends . . . well-mannered and they respect elders. I know I am bad . . . I couldn't be a good father…I am arrogant as you say . . . not as "cool" as you wanted me to be . . . but I am your dad. A dad who doesn't want to lose his son in the second innings of his life. I never managed to say it but . . . I love you and I missed you…I am proud to have a son like you. Yes, you did commit this mistake . . . but I am still proud of you,' he said, wiping away Varun's tears.

Varun's dad asked the girls why they took the risk of leaking a university paper. He was sure that Varun would not have wanted to cheat in an exam. It was then that Garima revealed the truth about her uncle who had blackmailed her. Varun's dad was completely taken aback by her uncle's villainy and assured Garima that she would get justice and that he would take proper action against her uncle. Garima thanked him for his concern.

Varun wanted to hug his dad. He had never seen him like this. Malvika understood that Varun wanted to be alone with his father, so she gestured to the others that they should leave. The three of them started walking towards the parking lot, leaving Varun and his dad alone. For a short span, neither spoke until Varun broke the ice.

'You commanded so much respect from those around you, but little did they know you had a poor, alcoholic upbringing. There is no doubt that you managed to build a life and a family even though the odds were stacked against you. You battled your own demons of depression and alcoholism but at times you got violent. Each violent step you took, took me away from you. I needed you when I took admission in Mumbai. Even I had no one but you,' said Varun.

'My greatest hope is for you to forgive me,' said his dad. 'Yes, I wanted you to join the army so that you would learn discipline. Trust me, you were the greatest gift God ever gave me. But I was frustrated. The loneliness killed me. You love to write poems, right? Today, I have written something for you. I don't know if it makes sense. But I am a bit shy to express my emotions verbally. Hence, I have written them down for you.'

Varun's dad handed him a letter. Varun glanced at his dad and opened it.

When you went away from me, I spent the entire morning, like so many mornings before, cursing myself for being distracted from my most sacred role by my need for perfection and my sense of duty and fear of rejection and desire for affirmation. And something inside me cracked.

I think it was my ego—the voice inside that told me that if I want to be good enough I had to look perfect, take care of everyone, win everybody over and be right all the time.

I want to apologize for behaving the way I did. I want to apologize for all of the ways I let my ego prevent me from being the kind of father you deserve. Every time you needed an embrace I responded with a slap. Every time, I demanded respect instead of earning it. Then I realized that even a father could take a son for granted which I shouldn't have. I'm sorry for every time I told you to be humble and then turned around and acted like losing was the end of the world. And I'm sorry for every time I didn't say "I'm sorry". I just want to give one piece of advice to you. Don't let anyone—including me—convince you that your worth is rooted in anything as short term as another person's opinion of you. Forgive me, if possible. Your dad needs you, as he is alone and lost.

Varun couldn't hold his tears back and without thinking for a second, he embraced his father like there was no tomorrow. His dad too wrapped his arms around him tightly.

'I just want to say one thing, Dad. The Indian army is not for the weak. Army people are not losers. They are winners and they protect us just like you protected me.' Varun saluted his dad proudly.

The fact is, anybody can be a father but it takes someone special to be a 'dad'.

Varun saw his dad off at the airport but not before telling him about his relationship with Malvika. For a change, his dad accepted it without asking too many questions and even blessed Malvika before leaving. Malvika was on cloud nine; blessings from her guy's father . . . what more could a girl ask for? If a guy is not comfortable holding his girl's hand in front of his parents, the girl should not let him hold her when they are alone. Varun was comfortable disclosing his relationship to his dad and thus taking it to the next level. Love is not always convenient, but if it is true love, it will outlast any strain, overcome any obstacle and grow consistently and exponentially for all eternity.

The next day, the two of them were sitting in Malvika's room, talking about everything they had faced in the past few days.

'I love it when I catch you looking at me, then you smile and look away,' Malvika said, pulling Varun's cheeks.

'I may not express this much but when I am with you, time is my biggest enemy.' As Varun lay on the bed, Malvika rested her head on his chest. Varun embraced her and kissed her forehead. A relationship should only be between two people and not include the world. Varun never cared about what others thought, he just loved her unconditionally. When he was shattered, disturbed or feeling lost, Malvika was the one to heal his deeply rooted wounds, and you never really forget the ones who touch your heart, regardless of whether they broke it or healed it.

'I want to make hard-core love to you right now,' Varun demanded.

'Now?'

Varun sealed her lips with a kiss. Soon their clothes were off. With each touch, Malvika's moans grew louder and Varun tried to shush her but couldn't. Soon she moved downwards, giving Varun the ultimate pleasure.

'The person who said there are no shortcuts to bliss surely didn't know the potential of a blow job.' Varun winked.

They continued their wild play until Ahana and Garima pushed the door open. Varun and Malvika grabbed a sheet to cover themselves up.

'At least lock your room. If you can't, then moan at a lower decibel level. Your voice is audible in the next block,' Ahana teased.

'You bitch, get lost. I will kill you,' Malvika yelled, throwing a pillow at her.

Varun simply shrunk under the blanket in embarrassment.

'Can I at least get into my boxers?' Varun asked shyly.

'Of course, dude. But we have already seen it all,' Ahana teased once again and went out with Garima.

Varun and Malvika looked at each other and couldn't stop smiling. After putting on their clothes, they went out to the living room. Both of them continued to blush until everyone burst out in peals of laughter.

'It's better to be caught red-handed by your friends than by the cops.' Varun smiled.

They fought like married couples, flirted like teenage lovers and behaved like best friends. Obviously they were meant to be! Love doesn't need to be perfect; it just needs to be true. Well, if your love is true then it's perfect.

'I am going to order a healthy breakfast today. I seriously need to eat healthy,' Malvika said.

'Bitch, please!' Ahana exclaimed.

'What? I am fucking serious, babe,' Malvika declared.

'Oh . . . fine. Varun and Ahana, you can join me in eating the BBQ chicken pizza that I just bought,' Garima whispered and immediately went inside Ahana's room to fetch it.

'What the . . .' Malvika began and before she completed her sentence, everyone ran inside Ahana's bedroom.

'Now don't change your words. I am not going to share it with you,' Ahana added.

'Calories don't count when it's your roommate's food.' Malvika winked.

'Such an ass you are.' Ahana threw a pillow at Malvika.

'You should not say no to pizza. Even they have "fillings".' Varun winked.

They had a huge fight over the last slice of pizza, but Varun snatched it first. Everyone looked at him with a sad face with the hope of getting a bite. Varun smiled and fed a bite to all the three girls. Friendship is about going out of your way to make the other person feel special. Some people get that, others don't. Varun, Malvika, Ahana and Garima didn't know each other a year ago but now they were the thickest of friends. The girls had brought Varun closer to his dad and Varun couldn't have asked for anything more in his life. Malvika too had found her true love who didn't want her to get married just after college but wanted her to be an independent girl who would make him proud. That was exactly what Malvika wanted from her life. Garima's demons wouldn't have been killed had she not met Varun, the guy with whom she was reluctant to share the apartment in the beginning. Ahana had learnt something about herself in the process. She had always thought that she was a complete socialite, going through life superficially with large groups of 'friends', never dreaming she could share such a strong bond with anyone. She had started believing in relationships and never wanted to be separated from these guys. She jokingly suggested that Garima and she should date each other so that all four of them could stay under one roof forever. They were friends 'four'ever. Whatever, whenever, wherever and however.

Good days give you happiness; bad ones teach you a lesson. All four of them had experienced their fair share of good and bad days, had survived and come out as winners. It's amazing how complete strangers can become such good friends in such a short span of time.

With Varun's father's help, Garima's uncle was finally put behind bars. Garima wanted to look her demon in the eye and finish it once and for all. Accompanied by her friends, she went to the prison cell where her uncle was locked up. To her surprise, her parents were there too.

Garima could no longer hold back her emotions.

'"You are so sexy, my puppy . . . you are one of a kind, my puppy." That's what you used to say to me, right?' Garima shouted, looking at her uncle, and added, 'You won't say this today? Or will you? In the bathroom? I used to shout in pain and you took advantage of me. Have you no shame?'

Garima's mother tried to console her but she pushed her away. Relationships never die a natural death. Her parents' indifference had given Garima the worst scars of her life. No matter how strong a girl is, sometimes all she needs is a hug.

'Such things do happen. Right? But now I am not going to be a weak person who just cries.'

'Okay. Let's be a little realistic,' her dad said, trying to comfort her.

'No. I don't want to be realistic,' Garima screamed at the top of her voice and added, 'I am the way I am. Don't expect me to change. Dad, you always warned me to be careful when I went out as there were people who would try to take advantage of me. Girls should always be careful.

Then why you didn't tell me that I have to be careful even inside my own house? To be careful with even my family? So please don't tell me to be realistic. I am not going to come home again. Ever.'

Saying this, Garima walked out of the prison with her friends close behind. She had made up her mind to live in Mumbai, no matter what.

Once outside, they all hugged each other and made a pact to always have each other's backs. Garima decided to leave behind the scars of her past and start her life all over again, but this time with her friends who were now her family. Friendship picks you up when the world lets you down!

Epilogue

Almost a year has passed since the MMS incident, and everyone has moved on with their lives. But they still live under one roof and still share the same unbreakable bond. They go lingerie shopping together, get drunk and sleep on the same bed, dance with each other in their night clothes, watch cheesy movies and cry on each other's shoulders, click countless selfies and eat several unhealthy pizzas.

One smile can start a friendship, one word can end a fight, one look can save a relationship and one person can change your life. Varun's life had changed since he had entered into a relationship with Malvika. She was the one who had ended the grudge that Varun had against his father, the result of which was the beginning of a healthy father–son relationship. Varun now treats his dad as a friend more than a father and shares all his problems with him. Sometimes, they even enjoy a drink or two together.

The case against the professor is still being fought in court and Varun appears, whenever summoned, to present his side of the story. Varun's dad is ready to support him to be an entrepreneur after his BSc.

Malvika still loves Varun passionately. She has introduced him to her parents who are extremely happy as Varun, apart from being responsible and mature, loves their daughter unconditionally. In our generation, having a loyal partner is a blessing. Now that she has found a partner, her parents are after her life to get married after graduation and Varun somehow has to convince them that he is the one who actually needs time to settle down. A girl's worst nightmare is when the guy she loves stops doing the things that made her fall in love with him. But Malvika has found a guy who never stops making her feel special. They do fight with each other every single day about their Facebook statuses, the last seen times on WhatsApp and so on but these fights are a part of every relationship. Love is when you piss each other off and want to kill each other but at the end of the day all you want is to be in your partner's arms. Malvika is a walking FM radio and Varun her addicted listener!

Ahana is still Malvika's BFF and they do insane things together. They still call unknown numbers after getting drunk and though they ask the same question, they get innovative answers every time. Clicking selfies and discussing which one to upload on Instagram still remains a hot topic for them. Though Ahana still prefers to stay single, she seeks relationship tips from Varun on how to get hold of a hot super stud. But more than finding herself a suitable match, she is extremely dedicated towards her dream of becoming one of the top fashion designers in the country. Sid's attempts to hurt her and win her back failed, as Ahana is not an easy catch. He still misses her but because he took her for granted, he has been left alone. One should not take people for granted, because we might end up missing them terribly tomorrow. However, Ahana's dad continues to take her for granted and she still craves his affection. He continues to deposit money in her bank account every month, but fails to deposit his love in her heart. She still hopes that one day he will come to his senses.

What about Garima? She has now moved on from the nightmares and always wears a happy smile on her face. Gradually, she has started living each moment of her life without any boundaries and considers Varun her brother. Sometimes all we need in life is that one special person who deeply inspires us and gives us the courage to be who we were meant to be. For her, Varun is that special person who stood up for her, and what his dad did, even her parents couldn't do. Her friends are her new family now.

This is not a love story; it's a story of lost innocence and teenage heartache in urban India. Often, depression overwhelms your heart, but you can't fix everything that goes wrong in your life. Sometimes you just have to make the best of the situation and move on.

Varun, Malvika, Ahana and Garima were indeed soulmates. Soulmates are not necessarily people who are in a romantic relationship; they are people who love each other and accept each other in spite of their shortcomings. They are people who bring out the best in you! Together Varun, Malvika, Ahana and Garima had proved their innocence. Now they could live life on their own terms—ready to face the challenges that the new day would bring with it. There are endings, but the stories continue . . .

Once in a while something or someone special comes along. This is when it's time to decide if the risks in life are worth taking. For them, the risk was worth it!

Acknowledgements

It takes hours to read a book but months to write one! During the writing phase, a few people become an inseparable part of the book. All the people I thank below were my strength while I was writing the book.

My millions of readers for their unflinching love and support. You mean the world to me!

Jasmine Sethi for being my soulmate and the only person to stand by my side whenever I felt dejected.

Dipika Tanna, my BFF and Jasmine's raita queen, for keeping me grounded and handling my tantrums.

Saurabh More, just because every time I mention his name, things work out for me.

Zankrut Oza for guiding me patiently and for his brotherly love whenever and wherever I need it.

Priyanka Dhasade for giving her valuable inputs whenever needed and Vivaksh Singh for his selfless assistance through thick and thin.

Neha Maheshwari and Mrunmayi Dhurandar for forcing their friends to read the book, even if they were not interested.

Apurva for her constant support and Sonja D'Silva for tolerating my nonsensical talk.

Shehzad Zaver and Zeeshan Panjwani for their warm love throughout and their precious time.

Diva Bhansali for saying flattering words all the time and Manvi Singh for her selfless support.

Manik Jaiswal and Narendra Singh for their open-handed promotions.

All the people who really matter—Mom, Dad and my sister Shweta—and my grandparents for believing in me. Love you all!

God for being kind to me when it comes to writing.

My extended family on Facebook and Twitter who selflessly promote the book.

Milee Ashwarya, Gurveen Chadha, Shruti Katoch and the whole team at Penguin Random House for their patience during the entire process of the book.

A Note on the Author

Sudeep Nagarkar has authored five bestselling novels—*Few Things Left Unsaid* (2011), *That's the Way We Met* (2012), *It Started with a Friend Request* (2013), *Sorry, You're Not My Type* (2014) and *You're the Password to My Life* (2014).

He is the recipient of the 2013 Youth Achievers' Award and has been featured on the *Forbes India* longlist of the most influential celebrities.

He also writes for television and has given guest lectures in various renowned institutes and organizations.

For more information about Sudeep, you can visit www.sudeepnagarkar.in or get in touch with him via his:

Facebook fan page: facebook.com/sudeepnagarkar

Facebook profile: facebook.com/nagarkarsudeep

Twitter handle: sudeep_nagarkar

Email: contact@sudeepnagarkar.in